BOOK

THE
CHRONICLES
OF
LEVI JONES

THE DISCOVERY

RYAN CRAWFORD

Fulton Books, Inc.
Meadville, PA

Published by Fulton Books 2021

ISBN 978-1-63710-474-3 (paperback)
ISBN 978-1-63710-475-0 (digital)

Printed in the United States of America

To my mother and best friend

Mom, without your love and encouragement, I would not be where I am today. You are the cornerstone of my success. I can never thank you enough.

Kristina Lockwood, please accept my deepest appreciation for all the kindness, love, and support you have given me. You will forever have a home in my heart.

CHAPTER ONE

It was early morning, and the warm air gently whisked along the coast. The calm waves of the ocean moved serenely in unison as the whitecaps gently broke against the rocky shoreline. The sunrise was oddly perfect as crisp shadows cast off the buildings, trees, and the bustling traffic while the morning awoke. Birds and waterfowl seemed to fly gracefully in slow motion across the skyline. Early risers were already out and about, walking their dogs along the park paths as they did every morning. The normal, mundane routine of life remained slow and relaxed as everyone carried on with their own lives. Business was usual at Binsley High School, the town's oldest public school building, which sat right on the coast with stunning views of the ocean seen from most classrooms. Students were carrying on with their friends in the busy hallways as they were making their way to class. Little did anyone suspect that something extraordinary, magical, and life-altering was about to happen in this small town.

It was a regular day in the multiple classrooms with students rifling through books and papers while carrying on conversations or looking at their cell phones. Most weren't even paying attention to the teachers or the lesson plans. The school bell rang earlier than usual, as it was a half day that started the three-day weekend. Mrs. Barren, one of the few English teachers, closed her textbook, which was lying on top of her desk, and said, "Okay, everyone, class is dismissed. Enjoy your weekend and study for next week's test." Every student in the room was full of excitement and cheered while gathering their books and bags and while starting to walk out to the school buses. Everyone could hear current music being played from various Bluetooth speakers and headphones. The hallway was filled with kids closing their lockers, and they could hear an unwavering enthusiasm, as most were excited to leave early that Thursday morning.

While the students were scrambling around the schoolyard looking for their bus or ride home, some staff members and chaperons were looking out toward the ocean beyond the school buses, viewing the ocean's horizon. They were not paying attention to the students or gentle waves of the ocean water; instead, they were focusing on what was forming in their field of vision. Something mammoth was brewing quickly as the bright sun lost its brilliance under the growing cloud cover. Most of the bus routes were local, but two buses had to travel to the far stretches of the rural parts of nearby towns.

As some time passed, school bus number 37, which traveled the farthest away from school, finally dropped off its remaining passengers. Levi Lumboss made his way off the school bus, which stopped in front of his house on the corner of Keelstrom Street. The front of his house faced the embankment, and the right side faced old wooden docks where schooners and fishing boats were tied off or anchored. Now off the bus, Levi stopped to wave to his friend. "I'll call you later," he said while walking to his front door, carrying his backpack. Only feet from his door, he paused and looked at the sky. He thought that his surroundings seemed way too quiet. *This was not the norm*, he thought, as this was usually a busy harbor town with sailors, dock crew, and shipwrights working. He watched a colony of seagulls along with some pelicans fly overhead, but it was as if nature pressed the mute button to quiet their normal noise. Small waves and ripples of water filled the sea, but silence fell upon the bay. He looked around the neighboring homes and didn't notice anyone outside or any activity of any kind. Levi noticed black clouds brewing in his scope, and even though something didn't feel right, he blew it off and returned to his happy thoughts of his early dismissal. While fetching his key, he checked the mailbox, grabbed the contents, and entered his home.

While walking into his old maritime home, he placed his backpack on the kitchen counter while looking through the mail. "Nothing for me," he said to himself, and he proceeded to the refrigerator to grab a snack. He was usually home alone for a short time as both his parents worked to support the family. As he plopped himself on the couch to watch some TV, he grabbed the remote control but wasn't able to push any buttons, as a loud crack of thunder startled him in the distance. Levi jumped off the couch and ran upstairs where he stood in front of the main upstairs window. He watched a forming storm cloud roll in rather quickly toward his house, which was in the town of Coralbrink.

The clouds were quickly developing and expanding in the sky, and it was growing darker outside. Within minutes, wind and heavy rains started. This sudden change in weather patterns skyrocketed the size and violence of the crashing waves in the harbor. Utility wires started whipping back and forth against the waterlogged power poles as intermittent sparks shot out of the dated electric transformers that powered the homes and businesses. The old fishing boats and schooners of the historic town of Coralbrink were being shaken from side to side, continually crashing against the dock as the thick ropes that secured them were being challenged.

Levi looked at the clock, wondering when his parents would return home from work. Levi's dad, Leo, was a copilot for a small private charter plane company that delivered fresh fish and seafood from Coralbrink to nearby states for higher-end restaurants that served fresh seafood daily. Leo was away delivering his cargo several hundred miles away and usually was home before the sunset of the evening. His mom, Lauren, worked part-time as a moderately successful travel agent in the neighboring town of Netinburg. Grabbing his cell phone, Levi continued to notice the increasing clouds, rain, and darkness spreading across the area as the window shutters opened and closed, slapping the side of the house. He tried sending a text message to his parents, only to receive an error message as the cell signal was intermittent.

Levi's mother, Lauren, was looking out the front window of the travel agent's office, also noticing that the weather was becoming dreadful. She unsuccessfully tried to call and text Levi, as her cell signal was also weak and intermittent. The winds in the town of Netinburg were becoming more intense and blew a large oak tree down, which blocked the entrance of the office. Authorities were shutting down the roads as the storm was growing. Police cars were carefully driving down the streets, avoiding a vast network of debris as they announced on their loud horns that everyone stayed indoors. Trying to stay calm, she said to her coworkers, "I can't get ahold of my son, and I've got to get home. I hope he is okay." Her peer tried to console her as she started sobbing. Operations in the office paused because it frustrated other travel agents, as the landline phones were down and so were their cell phones.

Meanwhile, Levi turned on the TV and tried flipping through several channels, but there was more interference on the screen than the weather forecast. During all the rapid growing commotion, there was a frantic banging knock at the front door. Levi ran down the stairs and looked through the peephole. There, clinging to a broken umbrella swaying back and forth while jumping up and down was his neighbor and best friend Jones Jackson. Jones stood as tall as Levi, although slightly more on the portly side. They coincidentally shared the same birthday date and age of thirteen. "Open the door, Levi! I'm getting soaked!" Jones cried out. Levi slowly opened the door while leaning against it so the wind wouldn't blow it open. Jones stumbled into the house, fighting to close the collapsed umbrella. "Good grief, where did this nasty weather come from?" he touted.

"There is a tremendous storm coming, and I can't get ahold of anyone. My cell has no signal, and the TV isn't working," Levi said with significant concern.

"My phone isn't working either," Jones complained as he shook the water from his outdated smartphone.

Levi continued, "I can't get ahold of my parents to see if they are okay."

"Well, my mom isn't home, and I can't call her either," said Jones, as he was the only child of a widowed parent.

Jones's father, Charlie, was a police officer who passed away in the line of duty. Jones's mother, Samantha, was also trying to reach him but had no luck. She was also a police officer in the town of Coralbrink. She herself became frustrated because her boss ordered her to shut down the roads and keep control with her fellow officers. With her police car parked in the middle of a street with its lights flashing, Samantha was on her cell phone trying to get ahold of Jones while her partner was out making sure all residents made their way to a safer location. She shook the phone and in frustration threw it in the passenger seat. She mumbled to herself, "Damn it. Well, I've taught Jones what to do in emergencies and I know he will be all right." *He's a smart kid*, Samantha thought, *I need to just keep calm and keep my wits about me.* With a worried look on her face, she returned her attention to her work. Everything was closing down, and she was so overwhelmed while busy with the damaging winds and fires that were flaring up.

"It's getting worse out there. I bet this will become a hurricane or something," Levi said as he stared out the front window.

"I'm nervous, Levi. What do we do?" inquired Jones.

Before Levi could answer, the frightening loud screech of the severe weather sirens roared. Its haunting tone shook the boys to the core. They ran from window to window in the house, looking outside as the rain grew heavier, and it continued to grow darker and darker. The few trees that once stood upright slumped sideways as the heavy winds continued to blow. Waves from the angry ocean pummeled the docks and shoreline.

Thunder rumbled and exploded in the sky as a brilliant burst of lightning struck a few feet from Levi's house, igniting a small part of the dock on fire. "We need to take cover!" said Levi as he noticed how close that lightning strike was to the house.

"Where do we go? Do we get in the closet or something?" Jones stated while casing the house for escape.

Debris were filling the air as the storm caused great destruction. Boats were flipping over and capsized. Parts of cars, bikes, and other equipment shot through the air as if launched from a cannon. Street lights and lamp posts were breaking away from their bases and were being damaged. Parts of buildings were ripping away from their secure foundations and flying in the air. The horrific sound of gale-force winds filled the air. With a thunderous boom and crash, one window in the front of Levi's house shattered inward as the gale force blew a boat oar through the air.

Blowing rain whipped the inside of the house as the change in air pressure started knocking pictures and collectibles off the wall while vibrating other windows. Levi caught in his peripheral vision several chunks of wood, metal, and wreckage flying around outside. The boys who were frightened and confused screamed while running through the house. "Oh my God, it's a hurricane! This way! Follow me!" yelled Levi as he grabbed Jones's hand and ran for the basement door. The basement was off limits per Levi's dad, but in this current situation, he disobeyed and pulled hard on the infrequently opened entry. Both boys rushed past the door with full adrenaline pumping.

They pulled the door shut as they made their way down the stairs to the basement. It was a dark, compact space filled with old moving boxes, some furniture, and an enormous tool chest. The only light that worked was a single bulb hanging from the ceiling, and even that was flickering. "What now?" said Jones as the boys could hear the destruction going on above them.

"I don't know. My father always told me to never come down here!" Levi bellowed as he looked around the basement. His dad always forbade him to go in the basement but never gave Levi a reason for that restriction. Meanwhile, little did the boys know that the hurricane would be the worst flash storm system in history, and its widespread fury was approaching the town.

The loud sounds of breaking, bending, cracking, shattering glass and projectile furniture slamming on the floor above drove the boys into a panic. The ground shook as it added a mild earthquake to the torment. The basement door blew open as wind, rain and debris started flying into the basement. The boys yelled as they scrambled for cover. "Over here!" Levi screamed as he motioned for Jones to follow him behind the large tool chest. They could hear sparks and explosions could as the hurricane slowly churned away at the defenseless town. The boys hunkered down in back of the tool chest. "I'm scared Jones! Oh my God!" cried Levi. The boys sat in the fetal position with their hands over their head as they huddled together.

The ceiling over the basement broke apart as the dim gray daylight from above poked its way through the timbers that made up the weakening floor. Boards started flying in the air with the force of a rocket. A huge timber log, likely from the town sawmill, burst through the basement ceiling with a brilliant explosion, slamming into the wall next to the boys. This broke through the concrete and plaster wall and exposed some old rotted boards behind. The winds grew more intense as the floor was ripping away from the foundation. Jones looked into the gap between the boards and noticed that there was an underground space behind the weathered planks that they could hide in. "Come on!" yelled Jones to Levi. He pushed and pulled on the boards till there was enough room to crawl through. The boys made their way behind the boards just as another log slammed into the tool chest, forcing it back and almost crushing them. The tool chest temporarily shielded the new entrance as tons of water and debris covered it while the hurricane ripped the house from its foundation. The boys were oblivious that the storm blew the remaining parts of the house out to sea.

CHAPTER TWO

Wet and scared, the boys were struggling to survive the situation. "Jeez, that was close!" said Levi as he checked on the condition of his dear friend. Behind the boards lay a dark narrow void. A rocky passage carved out of the stone and earth. The five-by-five square tunnel seemed to be dimly lit by a soft dull orange glow phosphorescence radiating from the rock formations. Levi and Jones were in awe as they pulled themselves to their knees.

"What is this place?" Jones said as he tried to calm himself down. They worked hard trying to return to the basement, but the heavy tool chest and fallen debris blocked the entrance. They also tried to ignore the sounds of destruction that they heard from the back of the vibrating tool chest. The force of the storm was still present as water was slowly weeping its way through the new entrance.

Levi tried once again to push his way back into the basement, but nothing moved. "I can't move it!" he cried out. "It's blocked!"

"Here, let me try," struggled Jones as he was out of breath from the attempt to push his way through.

They returned their attention to the passage ahead. Levi pulled out his semibroken phone with the cracked screen and turned on the flashlight. All they could make out were dense spiderwebs, dirt, scars on the rocks showing where they were struck with a pickax, and shadows of ancient minirock formations. "Where are we?" asked Levi with a frightened tone to his voice.

"I don't know. It looks like some old tunnel. Are you sure you're okay?" Jones inquired.

"I think so," Levi answered as they both wondered what to do next.

The boys noticed a noise in the foreground. Getting a grasp on the situation, Jones asked, "What's that sound?"

Levi was looking forward and shushed Jones as he tried to figure out where and what the noise was. It was dark, and they couldn't see over six feet in front of them. "It sounds like...it sounds like running water and lots of it. Maybe like a river or something," gasped Levi.

"River? How would there be a river down here, underground?" touted Jones.

"I don't know," replied Levi, "but we need to get out of here."

Slowly, the boys crawled on their hands and knees moving forward completely grossed out by spider webbing, crawling rats, and other menacing-looking pests that lived there. As they inched farther down the tunnel, the sound of the rushing water gradually became louder. The density of spiderwebs and rats increased the farther the boys crawled. "We've got to get out of here. Argh, I hate rats!" muttered Levi as the boys struggled to avoid the pests with the poor lighting of the passage.

They continued to crawl inch by inch, following the sound of water. Little did the boys know that they were descending deeper underground. "This is scary!" screeched Jones. Even with the low light from Levi's phone, the boys struggled to see in the distance aided by the dull glowing rocks of the tunnel.

"This must be a secret passageway," Levi whispered as he felt sick. Almost immediately the sound of the water stopped, and dead silence filled the tunnel. "W-w-w-what happened to the water?" he said. Levi said being cut off midquestion by a low, eerie, horrifying moan coming from the distance. The boys stopped dead in their tracks and became even more frightened as the moan became louder.

"Let's go back the other way!" shuddered Jones as the boys froze in panic.

"We can't! The exit is blocked. We have got to keep moving."

"Are you crazy!" interrupted Jones, "I'm not going down there. Didn't you hear that moan?"

"Well, we can't stay here," replied Levi.

Through the dark distance, the boys could see a small translucent light-green orb slowly float from the right side of the tunnel and into the left side while continuing to hear a scary low-tone moan. They closed their eyes in panic, then Levi said, "Come on! We have to keep going. We will die if we stay here." Just as quickly as the orb appeared, it disappeared, and the sound of water in the distance soon returned.

Meanwhile, the storm was intensifying, and the basement of the house was quickly filling up with storm water. The rest of the house and surrounding houses and businesses were being destroyed and swept away by the hurricane's explosive force. An intense exploding bang followed by a crack echoed through the tunnel followed by the sound of a massive amount of water flowing as it entered the tunnel through the entrance that the boys discovered behind the tool chest.

The boys, looking back from where they came, were horrified that the trickle of water turned into a gargantuan underground tsunami consuming the tunnel.

"Go! Go! Go!" screamed Jones as they tried to crawl faster into the dark tunnel.

Just as fast as they could crawl, the water quickly caught up with them, flipping them on their backs and washing them down the tunnel like a horrific waterslide into the abyss. Being thrown back and forth, Levi could not hold on to his phone as they both screamed continuously while the water carried them down the spooky shaft.

Their bodies were flung left and right as they slid even faster, as the water gained pressure and speed from the tunnel going deeper into the earth. Arms and legs were flailing back and forth as the water transported them down further into the darkness. Both Levi and Jones were yelling bloody murder at the top of their lungs as they struggled to breathe by keeping their heads above the water. The sounds of the raging water and the eerie moans of something frightening increased in volume. The tunnel swerved to the left and right as the boys' speed continued to increase with the rush of even more water. Suddenly, a blurry see-through green image of a head appeared out of nowhere and raced past the boys as their water ride to hell continued.

A loud frightening deep moan echoed from the head as it raced past the boys again, then disappeared back into the tunnel wall. The water seemed to slow down as the tunnel headed in a slight uphill direction. The head materialized out of nowhere again, keeping up with the boys this time. It opened its foul crooked mouth dripping with saliva while presenting its dirty and missing teeth as it moaned, "Go away!"

Frozen in panic, the boys couldn't speak a word as their water ride would soon be over. "Go back!" the head grumbled as its evil eyes rolled back in the head of its hideous scarred face. The head grew larger as it eased closer to the sliding boys. "This is your last warning!" screeched the head as it appeared to be almost foaming at the mouth as it disappeared back into the tunnel wall.

Suddenly, the sound of water was all that could be heard as the boys entered a glowing chamber at the end of the tunnel. And with a swooshing wave, the ground on which they were sliding disappeared, and the boys launched over a waterfall about twenty feet high, which poured into a large dark murky lagoon. They both yelled in terror as they plunged into the deep water. Both their heads soon surfaced. "Help! Levi! Help!" Jones screamed, trying to stay afloat. He wasn't a very strong swimmer, but neither was Levi. They grabbed each other and, with a frenzy of splashing and kicking, made their way to the shore of this open cavern.

They pulled themselves up on the flat rock area, coughing and gasping as they regained their breath. "Oh my God. Oh my God! What's happening?" cried out Levi.

"I don't know! I want to go home! This is a nightmare!" returned Jones.

"Are you okay?" Levi coughed up as he looked around this odd cavern, which glowed an ominous orange tinge. The strong flowing waterfall consumed the silence through this subterranean ancient grotto, which was filled with thousand-year-old stalactites and stalagmites.

"Wow, look at this place. How are we going to get out of here?" said Jones as he looked around.

The cavernous room was immense. It was large enough to return any echo twice and with more eerie delivery the second time around. The rock formations were thirty feet up, and the boys couldn't tell the width or diameter of the place because of the darkness of the outer edges. The waterfall, still flowing, had lost some pressure and slightly slowed down. There was a warm orange glow emanating from the formations, which kept the leeway from being dark. Levi and Jones pulled themselves to their feet and gazed at the ancient void. "Where the hell are we?" Levi said.

"Let's find a way out of here. I want to go home," said Jones, not realizing the storm had swept his home out to sea.

They didn't have a clue about what to do or where they could go. "We are trapped! There is no way out of here!" Levi sobbed as he looked back and forth for a solution. Panic took over the boys' emotions, and both cried. As fast as they dreaded the situation, something mysterious happened. The waterfall slowed down even further and then completely stopped running. The cavern was dead silent, then suddenly, the previously heard low, eerie moan started up again. The murky pool of water from which they crawled out of slowly emanated a green glow that was gradually intensifying when the translucent green orb they saw before appeared to swim around under the water and eventually made its way to the surface.

Both Levi and Jones froze in fear with their eyes and mouths wide open but unable to say anything. They had seen nothing paranormal in their lives. The orb casually broke the surface of the water and calmly floated toward the boys as the fright only grew on their faces. It made a chilling humming sound as it moved toward them. The spooky sphere hovered over the two and made crackling noises like a hot sparkler as it changed color from green to white. The light from the orb became intensely bright, bright enough where the boys had to cover their eyes. Slowly, the bright ball of energy transformed into unique shapes as it finally became the outline of a human body. The boys observed the spectacle as it formed, and it started looking like an old-time miner.

A dirty and battered leather helmet with a semicrushed and dented box mounted to it held an eerie flickering half candle for light. Dismal and muddy overalls with muck packed on boots completed the outfit on the apparition as it floated above the boys. Small crackling white shooting stars were slowly radiating around its body. As his torso was moving in slow motion, a gruff and mean-looking man with a thick mustache and greasy, scummy streaks of dirt covering his face held a heavy scowl as he stared down at poor Levi and Jones.

CHAPTER THREE

Levi and Jones were trembling in place with their eyes wide open and their jaws almost touching the ground. The glowing apparition did not break eye contact as it slowly opened its foul-looking mouth and spoke. "Who are you?" murmured the specter in a slow deep, low-vibrating voice.

The boys were shaking, but Jones stuttered, "I...I...am J-J-Jones...Jack...son, and t...this is L-Levi—"

The miner interrupted. "How did you get down here?"

"There i-i-is a storm, and we...we...were hiding in my b-basement...," Levi mustered up. "The wall w-was broken, and we found a t-tunnel, and we climbed in."

The miner's brow raised, and a heavier scowl replaced the temporary look of surprise. "*Silence! Why are you here?* You have entered a place where you should not be. This will be your ultimate resting place!" said the mining specter.

"N-no, please! We didn't mean to be here!" cried Levi as he pleaded with the ghost.

"We want to go home! Please don't hurt us!" said Jones in a shivering panic.

The ghost's eyes glowed with a neon green glare. "You have disturbed my grave, and now you will join me!" the ghost said as he hovered higher above the boys. Both boys fell to their knees.

"Please no! We want to leave, but we don't know how to get out of here!" yelled Levi.

"H-he's right. We want to leave. Please help us. Tell us how to get out of here!" Jones chimed in.

The miner fell silent and continued to glare at the boys as he hovered high above them. The scowl on his face grew angrier than before. The shooting stars emanating from the spirit's body increased as he put his hand on his ghostly chin, looking as if he were thinking about it. "You are the ones who have disturbed me! I should curse your souls for eternity," moaned the ghost, and he continued, "How could two kids find their way down here? You look too young to know about the legend. I may spare you from my fate only if you do something for me."

"What is it? Please tell us!" begged Levi.

"Whatever you want, we will do it. We just want to go home," pleaded Jones.

The ghost lethargically lowered itself down to the boys' level. His worn boots touched the ground, and he stood seven feet tall. He put his hands on his waist and squinted one eye as he stared down at the boys with the same scowl on his face. The boys, still on their knees, looked at the miner attentively in anticipation. The miner's bright glow softened slightly as he looked at the boys and, in his slow whispered speech, told of the legend. "Over one hundred and fifty years ago, when I was alive on this godforsaken earth, I accepted a job at a company called the Crenshaw Mining Company," said the miner as a dull white cloud formed to the side of him. Images formed on the cloud, and the boys could see the miner as he looked over a century ago. The images continued to change as the miner told his story.

"They hired me as the foremen of an elite group of men whose talents included deep excavation and exploration into the earth. The owner of the mining company was Orville Crenshaw, a renowned archaeologist and a very mysterious man who was rumored to study ancient black magic. He searched for many years for treasure and one day stumbled upon a map written on ancient parchment on his adventures and journeys around the world. The map supposedly leads to a powerful, inexplicable treasure. A treasure that contained unimaginable capabilities discovered by ancient peoples of many millennia ago."

The old man paused for a moment, then continued, "It was my job to find this treasure. Crenshaw gave me this small green amulet stone attached to this chain to wear around my neck as a promise of wonderful fortune and prosperity. He was a superstitious man, and I was told to never take it off or terrible luck would befall me and my men. He had me oversee my group of men charged with the task to dig a mine shaft to the treasure that's rumored to be buried deep in the earth by these ancient peoples."

The miner became silent and looked away with a look of disgust on his face, but continued, "I did not want to continue because my men were becoming exhausted, hurt, and dying as they slowly burrowed deeper and deeper. I became frustrated and asked myself why would we work so hard to dig deep into the earth and not know what we were looking for. Crenshaw was very cruel, mean, and secretive about everything. He promised me and my team untold wealth upon successfully finding whatever it was we were looking for. He said we would know what we were seeking when we found it." The miner returned his scowl to the boys.

"The old legend says that this treasure possesses no wealth but is magical." The boys paid intense attention to the images in the cloud but couldn't make out the blurry image of the treasure. "One day, while my men were removing rock and earth by filling mine-carts pulled by mule, a strange green mist filled the mine shafts. It was mysterious because the mist did not seem to come from anywhere but then, in the next second, just existed in the entire mine. Most of my men started passing out and died, and the others who were lucky enough to make it out soon died from exposure to this mysterious vapor.

"I rushed to the mine entrance, covering my face with my handkerchief to save more men, but soon I was overwhelmed and passed out. I fell down a deep shaft and was never seen again. When I became spiritually conscious of my death, I discovered that I had gained new abilities. You may call it magical powers, but I just view it as an extension of my body. It must have been the green amulet that cursed me to survive down here in the afterlife as I am very weak when in distance from the mine. Damn that Crenshaw! He must have known what would happen. Crenshaw, who was selfish, didn't want to suffer public humiliation and ridicule, so he soon hired more men to hide the mine by blowing up the entrance. It is said that he proclaimed 'If I can't have the power, no one will,' and with that, the mine entrance was destroyed and forgotten about.

"As time passed on, they built the town of Coralbrink on top of the mine and the burial sites of many of my men. I've been doomed to haunt this place for eternity. Apparently, you stumbled into one of the few air shafts that we dug for the mine. This is why you here," moaned the miner.

"W-what can we do to help you?" Levi said with concern.

The miner continued, "I cannot rest, and I am cursed to remain here until my job is over. You will need to continue where I left off. I don't know what the treasure looks like, but you have to find it, or you will join me in this earthly crypt till the end of time."

Levi looked at Jones and said, "W...we have no choice. We either do it or we will die."

Jones looked at Levi in shock and said, "Are you kidding me? We will die anyway! Oh my God, no! I don't want to die."

Levi comforted Jones and told the ghost that they would try.

"But how do we get out of here?" Jones said to the ghost.

"You have accepted the task, and if you fail, death will be your destiny." The miner wailed as he slowly raised his left arm and pointed.

"Your journey begins here. Good luck," moaned the ghost as he pointed to a section of the solid rock wall.

Jones looked at Levi and said, "What are we looking at? It's just a wall of rock."

Levi looked at the ghost and said, "I don't get it. How does this start with a wall?"

The miner let out a deep, horrific-sounding laugh and faded into the darkness of the water. Suddenly, a great underground earthquake shook the chamber the boys were in. Rock and debris fell from the top of the cavern like a horrific storm that turned the chamber upside down. Chunks of falling boulders destroyed the waterfall entrance and started filling up the dark lagoon. Levi and Jones tried to find cover behind a fallen boulder. "Ah, what's happening now?" Levi shuddered. A bright dot appeared on the wall near the top of the room. Starting at that point and in zig-zag fashion, it moved its way to the bottom of the wall. The rock cracked over the pattern that the bright dot made on the wall. With exceptional force, the wall spread apart by the sliding of massive slabs of rock where the crack had formed. The stones of the cavern-ous chamber's glow faded, and the area was dark. Once the debris cleared and the ground stopped shaking, a dull light emerged from behind those slabs, showing access to another chamber.

CHAPTER FOUR

Levi and Jones stood up, regained their composure, and dusted themselves off. "Are you okay?" Jones said as he was looking at the new opening that led deeper into their adventure.

"I think so. This is crazy," Levi touted as he was brushing rock and dirt out of his hair.

Upon gathering their fortitude, the boys stood next to each other looking at the new entrance with an ambient light beaming through it.

"Well, we better get going if we are getting out of here." Levi spoke to Jones as they stared in awe at the opening.

"Aren't you worried that we will not make it out of this?" answered Jones with a fearful look on his face.

"We can't go the other way, so let's be brave and do this." Levi motioned with his hand as he slowly started walking to the light. They worked their way through the rubble and made it to the entrance.

"Here goes nothing," Jones stated as Levi walked in front of him.

Walking past the slabs, they found themselves in another chamber. The ceiling wasn't as high as the previous area, but this chamber was a longer and narrower room. Old mining tools and broken equipment were strewn throughout this area. The boys slowly walked past and over objects that lay in front of them. Old pitchforks, shovels, mine car parts, and mining picks littered the area. "Look at all this stuff," Levi said in amazement of this historical find. Suddenly the boys stopped in fear.

"W-what's that over there?" Jones pointed as the boys noticed a skeleton lying on its back still dressed in tattered miner's clothes. An old miner's cap still covered the head.

"It must be one of the miners' men that died in here. Just try not to look at it," Levi said as he tried to keep his eyes in the opposite direction.

The boys trudged about five feet past the skeleton when they suddenly stopped in their tracks as they heard an eerie popping noise behind them. They both slowly turned around at the same time and saw that the skeleton they just past stood up and was facing them while pointing beyond them. "Ah!" they both screamed as the skeleton broke into pieces and became nothing more than a pile of bones and fabric. The boys turned back around and ran to the other side of the chamber while tripping over the historic objects that lay in their path.

"Oh, my gosh! Oh, my gosh. Jones! What the hell was that?" cried Levi in a panic. Jones could only try to mumble words as he was so frightened. It took a few minutes for them to stop shaking and breathe, but they calmed back down and proceeded.

There, at the end of the chamber was an old partially covered rusted mine track. Lying on its side was an old wooden mine car showing its age as it was nothing more than dried-out rotting wood held together by rusty bolts and metal trim. Levi and Jones looked to their right and noticed after about ten feet the track became mangled and out of alignment because of a rock slide from a collapsed part of the chamber. They looked to their left and saw the track leading to a downward direction into the darkness.

"It looks like this is the way out of here. Help me lift this up back onto the track," Levi stated as he investigated the mangled wreck.

"Are you crazy?" Jones said in amazement. "This thing doesn't even look safe. Who knows where these tracks lead? It's pitch-black down there!"

Levi responded, "Do you have any other ideas because last time I looked, the only way out was haunted by a ghost and destroyed by an earthquake?"

"You have a point. Come on, let's try to get this thing upright." Jones struggled to say as they attempted to lift the mine car right side up on the track. After some hoisting and grunting, they finally positioned the rickety mine car back onto the track.

"We should get in and go," Levi suggested.

"Wait!" blared Jones.

"What?" Levi answered.

"I...I have to go to the bathroom," Jones said with embarrassment.

"Well, go back into that room and go. I'll wait for you here," Levi suggested.

Jones reluctantly walked back into the room and was looking for a place to pee. He found a spot close to the pile of bones. "Don't look at it. Don't look at it," Jones said to himself as he was relieving himself on the wall. Suddenly, he heard that eerie popping again, and he stared straight at the wall as his eyes almost popped out of his head. He zipped up and slowly looked over his shoulder. There was the skeleton, all put back together with an angry look on the skull. "Ah!" Jones screamed as he ran toward the mine car except in this moment, the skeleton started chasing poor Jones.

Meanwhile, Levi had climbed inside of the mine car and was trying to figure out the next move when he heard Jones screaming from the distance. Jones was profusely sweating while running as fast as he could. It didn't matter how fast he ran because the skeleton was right behind him and gaining. Jones turned the corner yelling, "Go, Go, Go!" Before Levi could understand what was going on, Jones leaped in the air and crash-landed inside of the mine car. That was enough force to push it down the track. They both looked behind themselves and saw the skeleton collapse into a pile of bones again. This was right before the mine car plunged downhill into the darkness.

The boys started screaming at the top of their lungs. They both squatted down and tried to hold on to anything to keep themselves from flying out of the mine car. They experienced zero Gs as the car seemed to keep plunging in a downward pace. Like a horrifying broken roller coaster ride, the mine car traveled along the rusty and crooked track, barely clinging to it as it went over and under the mined-out path in the near-dark. As the runaway carriage picked up speed, it would often tip on only two wheels as it turned corners.

Sparks shot out of the wheels as if they attached firecrackers to them. Through its travel, the mine car entered enormous caverns containing many skeletons, pieced-out bones, old crushed helmets, chunks of ore sticking out of the rock walls, and mining-type machinery. Almost instantly, the runaway ride would then sharply turn through small carved-out corridors. Left and right, up and down, the mine car traveled as if they built the track through an endless maze of cave tunnels. The cart slowed down as it finally reached a lofty peak of the tracks that crested over a large, deep open area of the mine. It came to a complete stop and rested at the very top as if on a level teeter-totter. Levi poked his head above the top of the mine car. "W-w-what happened? Why did we stop?"

"I...I don't know. Is this thing over yet?" Jones replied.

"We are stuck. We need to get out of this thing," said Levi as he panicked.

They could hear drips of water and groups of bats in the background. They didn't realize that one good lean forward would continue their ride. "I'm scared. I want to get off this thing," Jones was saying when he suddenly burst into a deep sneeze, which was hard enough to jerk the car forward.

"Jones! No!" Levi yelled as they went over the peak.

The mine car continued to speed up while almost plummeting off the track into the dark depths while both boys screamed in terror. The grinding metal and hammering, clanking noises almost drowned out the boys' cries for help. The bolts of the rusted transport were vibrating and starting to shake loose. After every sharp turn, they dove past colonies of bats that swarmed over their heads. Dense spiderwebs and roots hung from above and protruded from the walls of the jagged tunnels. Broken mining cars that were thrown from the track and wooden barrels were spread out through this coaster of a hell ride.

Skeletons of all the fallen miners were still in position, holding their tools as if they continued mining in their afterlife. Small waterfalls seeped through the cracks from much of the tunnel. Just when the boys were about to lose their grip and fly out of the vehicle, it entered a large mysterious cavern, which glowed a bright purple color as light emitted from the underground lakes that surrounded both sides of the track. Levi looked through one of the many cracks of the rotted wood. It looked like a different world as purple light glowed from the rock formations that were submerged or surrounded the vast bodies of water. Everything was silent except the squeak from the rusty wheels of the makeshift coaster car.

The boys mysteriously slowed down, not stopping on the track that was following a very narrow rocky path. The boys didn't dare try to get out of the mine car because they would fall right into the glowing purple water. Oddly enough, the track was perfectly level, but the car kept moving forward slowly. They poked their heads up over the edge of the mine car just enough where they could observe broken old crates and the bones of fallen miners as they crept down the track. "W-w-where are w-we?" Levi could barely utter as he tried to catch his breath.

"I...I don't know." Jones continued as he was looking around, "Look at all the d-d-d-dead guys, Levi. There must have been hundreds of people working down here."

Levi looked around and said, "Please, please, please don't come to life." As he was thinking about what recently happened at the beginning of this journey, gigantic spiders were hanging down from their webs high above the track. The mine car suddenly screeched to a dead halt right in the center of what seemed to be a crumbling narrow wooden bridge that was built over different elevations of rock formations. The bridge was only a few feet above the water and did not look like it could carry any more cargo over it.

Total silence filled the chamber, and the water was still. "What are we supposed to do now?" Jones asked his traveling companion.

"I don't know. We can't get out of this mine car. We will end up—" The immediate bubbling action of the water surrounding both sides of the track interrupted Levi. Bubbles rose rapidly from the pool of water at a consistently increasing pace. Smoke rose with the bubbles as the water boiled.

"What the?" Jones yelled out. The water continued to get hotter and hotter, filling the area with steam.

"We've got to get out of here!" Levi yelled.

The boys were both panicking, looking around the rock-laden area frantically for a solution. Suddenly, a circular green orb of light shone in the water close to the mine car. In what seemed to be a slow dramatic fashion, the ghost miner's image materialized and appeared to rise out of the boiling water and hovered a few feet above the mine car. He still had an angry scowl on his face as he glared at the boys. "What's taking you so long?" moaned the miner as if displeased with the boys' progress this early in the adventure.

"We are stuck on this track! There is no way we can move!" retorted Jones, thinking that this miner was blind not seeing their predicament. The miner looked more aggravated by the second, then he slowly descended back into the boiling water, disappearing under the steam cover.

"What the heck was that?" Levi said and continued, "What does he think we can do without being stuck here?"

Soon after Levi's statement, the water stopped boiling, and silence fell upon the chamber again. The boys both sat back down in the damaged rail buggy and tried to figure out what to do. Instantly, eerie popping noises broke their mumbling ideas to each other. Jones looked at Levi with his eyes wide open. "Oh no! It can't be. Not again!" Jones said as he lifted his head up high enough for his eyes to look over the back of the car. His eyes bugged out of his head as he stuttered while slapping Levi's shoulder for his attention.

"What do you w..." was all Levi could say as he turned around and saw what Jones was shocked by.

There, standing on the track peering down at the boys was a huge ghostly skeleton with glowing flames for eyes and an evil grin on its face. It stood eight feet tall, and its dirty bones appeared to be attached by some magical force as every joint glowed white with little sparks emitting from them. "Ah!" the boys wailed in horror. As fast as they screamed, the skeleton grabbed the back of the mine car and pushed it very hard. The skeleton stayed right behind the car, pushing it uphill as its jaw hung open. A loud horrifying laugh came from the bony specter as it was pushing so hard that its lower body was running to keep up with the top portion.

Once again, screeching and sparks erupted from the old mine car as it went up over a rocky boulder. The ride became increasingly bumpier and violent as they rode down the rickety track. The boys saw a break in the track, but the spooky specter pushed even faster, making the mine car jump the track before the break and land precisely where the track continued. This experience was becoming even more dangerous, as the track was twisting and become uneven. Both Levi and Jones were feeling sick to the stomach. Levi was about to vomit when his attention was commanded by more beastly bats flying out of every direction in the darkness. The boys tried very hard to stay in the coco pan while dodging diving bats and the sudden twist of the rickety tracks. The ground was disappearing as huge voids and open pits were exposed under the track. The track continued to twist and turn as the wheels of the mine car lost its grip and direction. The boys unfortunately realized that the mine car would not stay on the track for long.

"Hold on! This thing is falling apart!" a horrified Levi screamed. Jones was silent as he watched the end of the track approaching in the distance. The skeleton laughed even louder as it was not slowing down. After passing a deep underground ravine, the skeleton suddenly let go. The boys looked back and saw the bones collapse and fall into the ravine. They quickly returned their attention to the front of the terror ride where the track was about to end.

"Oh no! Dead end coming! Duck!" Jones screamed. The mine car soon slammed into an old dried out rail car stop made of wood, which broke apart when the car hit it. The boys were thrown from the mine car and launched into the air. With their arms and legs thrashing everywhere and with screams of horror, they both landed in a gigantic pile of oversized feathers.

The wooden cart lay shattered into many broken pieces. Cracked wood, bent trim, and hardware were everywhere. Smoke rose from the hot overworked wheels. The boys, dazed from the impact, were trying to regain composure while lying on the tremendous collection of feathers that broke their fall as they weren't seriously hurt. Still wet and covered in dirt, they discovered that some of their clothes were torn from the adventure so far. Briefly, the boys caught their breath while coughing and dusting themselves off. Both of them always felt a sense of dread because everywhere that they have ventured so far was always dark and a fresh surprise always seemed to be around the corner. They wondered where they were now as this unfamiliar area differed from the others.

It was breezy in this unknown area while dimly lit by the eerie glow from the phosphorescent rocks that surrounded the area. Thick thatches of daddy longlegs webbing and nesting material were scattered through the musty-smelling expanse. The ceiling was not visible in this area, as the higher the boys tried to look, the darker and more void it became. Levi and Jones could see nothing more than darkness behind them as if everything that happened before just disappeared. "Where are we? How can there be wind be blowing underground?" asked Jones.

"I don't know," answered a puzzled Levi.

"Now where are we supposed to go?" Jones continued, "If we had that map the crazy ol' miner guy was talking about, maybe we could find the treasure and go home."

"What is this that we landed on?" Levi said, looking around at the vast bed of feathers they were sitting in.

"I don't know, but it sure smells in here!" Jones bellowed as he tried to get off the pile.

"Look at the size of these things," Levi said, examining the nest closer and feeling the length of the feathers.

"I've never seen feathers like this before," Jones said as he looked closer himself, then continued," But what has feathers this big?" Almost instantly, the boys heard a loud, haunting, powerful shriek in the distance that pierced the near silence.

"W-w-what is that?" Levi said with alarm. The shrieking was getting louder and echoed in the darkness with great vibration.

"I don't know what that is, but we have got to get out of here!" yelled Jones. The breeze increased, and mammoth-flapping and aerial-floundering noises killed the silence.

"No...no..., there is no way that can be what I'm thinking," Levi said before he was cut off by two big glowing bloodshot eyeballs appearing in the darkness above. The shriek became intensely loud, and the eyeballs were growing in size as out of the darkness a huge, dirty, and disfigured vulture-like bird creature was descending. It possessed a strong thick heavy beak, blood-soaked feathers, and scars from past fights. Like heavy hail raining from the sky, the bird had the boys on its sight.

"Run!" shouted Jones as the boys struggled to climb out of the feathery nest. They freed themselves from the nest and ran down to a nearby tunnel with the bird creature flying behind them.

The shaft was not as wide or high enough for the bird to move, so when the creature's wings hit the sides of the tunnel, tons of rock and debris were falling everywhere, destroying the path behind the boys. "Run, run, run!" Jones screamed as the bird was in full-speed chase destroying everything behind the boys. The wind created by the bird's wings made running difficult for the youngsters as if something trapped them in a vacuum cyclone. Levi could see far ahead and noticed the tunnel would end.

"Jones! When I count to three, dive on the ground!" Levi blurted, running out of breath.

"W-w-what? But—" Jones cried out as he was interrupted by Levi's count down.

"One...two...three!" Levi screamed as he and Jones instantly dove to the ground, landing on their stomachs. Immediately as they hit the ground, the creature flew over them like a passenger jet that was too close to the ground and slammed into the dead end, causing the rock wall to explode and crumble. Chunks of rock and dirt were flying and falling everywhere. The resulting noise and ground shaking was like the earthquake the boys experienced earlier. The now extremely disfigured creature disappeared into the darkness below as its crash opened an entrance to another unknown area for the boys.

"Jones! Jones! Are you okay?" Levi called out. Jones sat up, shaking the dust and rock off his head. Before he could talk, he was spitting pebbles and dirt out of his mouth.

"Ugh! Yeah, I guess so," Jones stated as he tried to stand up. "What in the hell was that thing? How did a bird get underground? Can you still see it?" Jones asked Levi while catching his breath.

"I see nothing at all. How big is this place?" questioned Levi, looking at the new entrance. "We are underground. How can this be? It doesn't make sense. Something is not right. How can these things be real?" continued Levi as frustration grew on his face.

Like watching a steam boiler build up too much pressure and exploding, Jones couldn't take anymore. "Damn it! I can't deal with this anymore!" Jones belted out. "Where is that miner? I would love to tell him off!" Jones continued to scream.

"Calm down." Levi said, trying to relax Jones.

"No! It's not right! We don't deserve this. We didn't do anything, and now we are stuck down here! I want to go home, and we don't even know where to go or what we are doing!" Jones continued to elevate his tantrum. "Where are you, miner? You did this to us! Get over here now!"

Silence immediately filled the area. "Oh no. What did you do?" Levi asked.

Suddenly, a loud moan increasing in volume filled the tunnel. The boys looked at the new entrance as it started glowing green from below where the bird disappeared. Another translucent green orb slowly floated from the depths and hovered over the boys once again.

"I'm not afraid of you anymore!" Jones yelled out as he continued to feel brave. "Why are you doing this to us? We don't know where to go or what we are looking for! I'm not moving another inch till you explain yourself!" Jones stood up tall and straight and, for the first time in his life, had no fear on his face. The orb hovered in front of Jones and glowed with a bright white light, which made both boys shield their eyes. In the blink of an eye, the spectral miner appeared with a heavy scowl still on his face, and he was in a dead stare down with Jones.

"Jones, back up!" Levi shouted.

"No! He brought us here, and he needs to explain himself!" Jones said, standing firm.

The miner leaned forward while staring at Jones with his mouth dripping drool and said, "How dare you question me! You want to know what's happening? I will show you!" the miner slowly said as he raised his arm and snapped his fingers. Bright flashes and crackling stars fell from the miner's hand and floated in Jones's direction.

CHAPTER FIVE

After the crackling stopped, when the miner snapped his fingers, a brilliant but soft blue flame emitted from his hand and floated toward Jones with the remaining sparkling stars in the air. It looked like a flame traveling on an invisible candle. The boys were frozen in place. The blue flame surrounded and engulfed Jones as his eyes were wide open and his teeth were clinched. He looked as if he were shivering, but he wasn't cold. The flame wasn't burning him, as it looked more like it was burning around him. His hands were held down by his sides with his palms up and fingers in a gripping shape. He levitated a couple of feet off the ground. His eyes glowed a super bright white gleam and glowing blue orbs appeared and hovered above each hand. The orbs looked like beaming blue water balls with waves constantly moving in and around it. It became instantly windy in that compact space.

"OMG! What's happening?" yelled Levi as he freaked out at the spectacle. "Jones! Jones! Wake up! Let him go!" continued Levi as he watched his friend's transformation.

The miner turned and looked at Levi. "Silence! He wanted to know what's going on, so he will find out right now. I'm engraving the contents of the map to his mind," murmured the miner as his eyes glowed with flames. Jones looked possessed as he floated a few feet up the air. Visible waves radiated from the miner's gnarled fingers, and with a movement of the miner's hand, most of the history of the mine and what was known about the treasure was spiritually transferred into Jones's head. A look of horror came over Jones's face as he whipped his head back and forth in fear.

"What are you doing to him?" demanded Levi.

The miner looked at Levi and moaned, "He's feeling how I died."

Jones moaned in pain.

"Leave him alone!" cried Levi as he watched his friend in pain. With another wave of the miner's hand, Jones slowly returned to the ground, and most of the blue flames that covered his eyes floated back into the miner's hand. The wind halted. Jones lay in front of Levi, almost lifeless.

"He now knows what's on the map. No more stalling! Get going or suffer my fate!" insisted the ghostly specter. He let out a big exhale, then he eerily disappeared back into the ground.

When the specter disappeared, Levi kneeled down in front of Jones, shaking him. "Wake up! Wake up!" Levi cried as he continued to try to wake his friend. After appearing lifeless for several seconds, Jones finally moaned for a second, then came to.

"W-what h-happened?" Jones said in a daze.

Panicking, Levi said, "You were floating. You were floating and on fire... Blue..."

"W...what? Blue what?" Jones said as Levi noticed something different about his friend.

"What's wrong with your eyes?" a panicked Levi said as he noticed that Jones had small faint light-blue flames in the center of both eyes.

"What do you mean what's wrong with my eyes? I've never seen clearer in my life," Jones responded as he made his way back up to his feet.

"You have fire in your eyes." Levi pointed out in amazement.

"What? You're nuts," Jones said, shrugging the comment off.

Levi then noticed something glowing under Jones's shirt. "What's that?" he said, pointing to Jones's chest.

"What's what?" Jones said as he looked down and noticed a green glow from beneath his shirt. He pulled on the necklace that mysteriously materialized around his neck and made a shocking discovery. "It's a green amulet! One like that miner told us he had to wear," Jones presumed.

"Where did it come from?" Levi said, ever so puzzled.

Jones tried to take it off, but he couldn't. Some odd power from the amulet kept it around his neck. "I can't take this damn thing off. Maybe it will bring us luck like it did the miner. Although being stuck down here doesn't seem too lucky to me. Ugh. Oh well, come on, we've got to go this way," Jones said as he was making his way to the next area.

"You're right. I really doubt any luck can come from that thing. Wait!" Levi shouted as Jones stopped and looked back. "How do you know where you're going?"

"I don't know," said Jones. "I just have a feeling."

Levi stared at his friend and thought that Jones seemed oddly calm and rational. *Isn't he afraid?* Levi thought.

Jones, looking almost half-conscious and in a zombielike trance, invited Levi to follow him through the new passage that the bird creature created.

"Are you okay?" Levi said, looking concerned about Jones's new disposition.

Jones just smiled at Levi and said, "I'm quite well, Levi."

Poor Levi just shook his head and followed Jones as they climbed over the fallen boulders, rubble, and rock. As they entered the new area, they noticed a huge dark gorge containing sharp, jagged pointed rocks that seemed to disappear the farther down it went. A rope bridge crossed over the very center of the gorge. Looking up, they noticed nothing but black space, just as they did in the feather nest. The boys descended the jagged, broken rocks of the remaining damaged passage and stood on a platform where one end of the bridge was attached.

Ancient broken artifacts containing hieroglyphics and weird writing were all over the place, and some mining equipment surrounded the platform. Two bamboo-type poles held torches that burned dried feathers that were tied together with twine on either side of the bridge. The torches were not lit, but as soon as Jones looked at them, they ignited with the same light-blue flames as Jones's eyes. The miniblaze of the torches lit the area with good ambient light. Jones stopped in front of the rope bridge that tied the platform they were on to the other side, which appeared to be home to some rock wall with different-shaped holes in it and a stone pedestal that sat in front of it. The rope bridge looked as if it were barely secure, being only fastened to a large bamboo post. It was falling apart as the dried-up braiding of vines and rotting bamboo floor gave hint that it wouldn't hold the boys. Levi watched as Jones just stared at the bridge as if he were in some amazed trance.

"Well, do we cross it?" Levi asked, as he knew Jones had the map information within himself.

Without blinking an eye, Jones said, "Yes."

"You first," Levi insisted.

Jones slowly placed one foot at a time on the bamboo flooring. The bridge swayed back and forth while making creaky sounds from the pressure of Jones's feet upon it. Levi was too scared to move. Jones crossed the overpass slowly as if unconsciously ignoring the deteriorating condition of the bridge. Levi continued to watch his friend as he made it to the center of the bridge. Jones's eyes were fixed on the next platform, and he didn't blink an eye. They could hear the braided rope pulling and stretching under the pressure. "Careful, Jones!" Levi yelled out as it echoed to the pit below. One foot in front of the next as the bridge swayed, Jones finally made it to the other end. He turned around and stared at Levi with a silent, blank grin.

"Your turn," Jones said, waving his hand gesturing for Levi to cross.

Showing all his nerves, Levi placed one foot on the bridge. The sounds of cracking bamboo became stronger as he placed his other foot in front of the next. The old span swayed from side to side, and the torches started to crackle and flicker. Levi started to make his way across the bridge, carefully watching where he stepped, and unlike Jones's journey, the sounds of the weakening bridge became much louder. Levi made it to the center of the bridge when he heard a horrifying howling screech noise from the black depths beneath him. "What the?" Levi said as he looked over the rope handle and down. A gust of wind blew from the depths, and Levi saw two big bloodshot eyes open and glow from below.

Before he could get gather his thoughts, he heard intense flapping noises as the wind increased. Levi stood straight up and tried to make his way across the rest of the bridge while it swayed back and forth more violently from the wind from below. Misstepping in his panic, the bamboo flooring was breaking beneath his feet. The screeching became louder, and the wind rapidly became more intense as Levi struggled to make the final few feet off the bridge while breaking more bamboo. "No, no, no. Come on, Levi, you can do it," Jones mumbled to himself.

Just as he was at the end of the bridge, Levi jumped forward onto the platform that Jones was on, and in that instant, the evil vulture-like creature howled from the depths of the black pit, hitting the bridge and destroying it as it flew upward. The explosion and debris from the bridge caused both boys to fall backward and made Levi shriek hysterically. The torches at the beginning of the bridge blew out, and the only source of light came from the torches where the boys stood. The winged creature disappeared in the blackness above. It turned around and dove back into the black of the pit while making an evil, horrible screech.

Levi looked at Jones, who was perfectly still and grinning while looking straight forward. "Ah! Did you...see...bird...bridge..." A frantic Levi was trying to point out to Jones. After forcing himself to breathe slowly and calm down, Levi saw that there was no way back across the pit. Jones turned around and stared at the wall with the distinct shapes, and Levi soon followed suit.

The bamboo torches lethargically lit the rock wall, which was covered with thin spiderwebs and vines. It had five different-shaped holes cut into it. In front of the wall sat a flat rock resting on two other stones that elevated the flat stone two feet from the ground. It looked like a makeshift table of sorts. On the flat surface lay five different-shaped rocks that were not the same shapes as the ones on the wall and a piece of shiny metal that looked like a small antique hand mirror. Levi slowly walked up to the wall and moved the vines to the side while he wiped away most of the spiderwebs. Levi said, "What is this? Is this a puzzle? I don't understand it."

Jones said with the same blank look on his face, "This is how we continue our journey. We must fit the rocks into the correct hole, and when complete, something miraculous will happen."

"But how?" Levi interrupted. "The rocks don't match the shape of the holes."

Jones repeated, "We must fit the rocks into the correct hole, and something miraculous will happen."

"What is this shiny metal for?" Levi chimed in as he sifted through the contents on the rock table.

"We must fit the rocks into the correct hole, and something miraculous will happen," Jones repeated.

"I don't know what you mean!" Levi yelled to Jones, who was still staring at the wall.

In his frustration, Levi picked up one of the rock puzzle pieces and tried to put it in one of the special-shaped holes. "See! It doesn't fit!" Levi said, holding the wrong piece over a hole. Immediately after his statement, the ground shook. "N-now what?" Levi said, looking around as the ground shook so hard a chunk of the platform they were standing on broke off and fell into the black pit. The shaking soon stopped.

"I wouldn't put the wrong rock into the wrong hole again, or our journey will be over soon." Jones said with a calm, trancelike demeanor.

"What the hell is wrong with you?" Levi sputtered while putting the rock puzzle piece back where he found it. "This is crazy, and you're so calm. What did that miner do to you?"

As Jones stood there quietly staring at the puzzle, Levi started pacing around and was growing in frustration. "We will never get out of here!" Levi said as he threw a fit and knocked the metal off the platform. "We are going to die!" Levi cried as he fell to his knees weeping. "We will die!" Levi said again as he sat down and crossed his legs. He sat there and cried and looked around his future tomb when he caught a glimpse of the reflection of the wall through the shiny piece of metal that landed sitting in a vertical position. "What the?" Levi bellowed as he looked at the metal piece. Upon picking up the shiny metal and looking at the reflection of the wall, the holes' shapes changed to the shape of the rocks on the platform. "I've got it! I've got it!" Levi screamed with excitement. He jumped to his feet and carefully placed the first stone while looking at the metal simultaneously.

Across the darkness, two torches suddenly ignited, and they heard a large grinding noise. On the other side of the pit, the beginnings of a bridge appeared. "Jones, look over there!" as he pointed to their escape route. Levi picked up the second stone and, again looking at the reflection of the wall in the piece of metal, placed it in the correct hole. They heard yet another grinding noise, and more bridge appeared to swing out toward the boys. Jones's blank grin disappeared for a second as he cheered on his pal as he was solving the puzzle.

Levi grabbed another stone, and when he took it from the table, a small button underneath it popped up. A hole in a nearby wall had a round stone slab roll away from it where suddenly hundreds of bats flew out of it, knocking Levi forward, and he accidentally placed the stone puzzle piece to the wrong hole. The ground started shaking again, more violently than before, and Jones and Levi tried to brace themselves as another enormous chunk of platform cracked and fell into the black pit. While dodging the bats, the boys were running out of space to stand, but you wouldn't know it by the calm look on Jones's face as he said, "Let's continue."

When the ground stopped shaking, Levi, stricken with panic, slowly stood back up and continued to work through the puzzle. "That was crazy! Careful, Jones! We are running out of room. I'm assuming that when I insert all five rocks, this bridge will free us!" Levi said as he inserted the third and then the fourth stone. By this time the bridge was almost across the pit and just about connected to the remaining platform the boys stood on. Carefully, Levi picked up the fifth piece, but it slipped from his hands and fell to the ground, breaking in half. "Oh no!" Levi shouted. In his great annoyance, he looked at the bridge and noticed that it wasn't close enough to the platform to even jump on, so he had to finish the puzzle. He picked up the two broken halves, held them together and shoved them into the correct hole. Almost instantly, the ground shook as the bridge completed its connection. Rocks and debris fell from above, and the remaining platform the boys stood on was cracking and falling away. "Run!" Levi said as he grabbed Jones's hand and started pulling him across the bridge.

As soon as they were near the middle of the bridge, additional enormous boulders fell and destroyed what was left of the puzzle platform, knocking it down into the black pit below. The ground continued to shake while boulders still descended downward and now were destroying the new bridge one section at a time.

"Come on, Jones! Run!" Levi yelled while still pulling on Jones's hand. Right as Levi and Jones took their last footstep on the bridge, mammoth boulders fell as if in slow motion from the darkness above, landed on the bridge, and destroyed the rest of it. The violent shaking soon stopped. "Argh!" Levi yelled as it made him fearful from the events. The boys just stared at the dark pit and where the bridge used to be.

"That was close," Jones said in a calm voice. "We must continue."

"W-we almost died! Aren't you scared?" Levi interjected.

"Very much so." Jones responded in a quiet, calm monotone voice. Jones turned around followed by Levi, only to see their next challenge.

"Oh, come on! When is this going to end? We have to go in there?" Levi said to Jones as he pointed forward.

There in front of the boys was an entry built from large flat slabs of stone. The torches next to what was left of the bridge calmly lit the area. It was a shallow opening that had two tunnels bored after it. Both tunnels were round and had the scars of pitchforks embedded into them. One tunnel was dug traveling to the left, and the other was dug out heading to the right. Sitting in the center of the two pathways was a small pile of broken wooden boxes and barrels. Sitting on top of those was a partially dressed skeleton with a miner's hat on. Covered in cobwebs, the spooky skull had a snake slithering out of its eye. The way the remains were positioned, this corpse met his doom like the miners before him.

"Oh, gross," Levi said in disgust, focusing on the grizzly site. The bony left arm was elevated by resting on the barrels at the top of the pile, while his hand appeared to be pointing to the right. In the left hand, there appeared to be a bamboo torch. "Wow, that guy is scary. Which one do we choose?" Levi said, looking at Jones for answers.

"This is a perplexing predicament." Jones replied.

"Perplexing? Predicament? Since when do you talk like that?" Levi mentioned, chuckling to himself as he watched the snake slither away. "Well, this guy seems to point to the right tunnel, so let's try it," Levi said. After those words were spoken, the torch mysteriously lit and gave off a dim flickering flame of light. Levi hesitated to grab the torch, as he was crept out by the skeleton, but he did so. They slowly started walking down the right tunnel.

This area was dug out and held together by thick timber columns that kept the ceiling from caving in on the tunnel's jagged, edged walls. Just like the areas before, this tunnel was loaded with mounds of broken clay pots, partially mined ore, and different-colored mineral deposits. Broken mine car rails started in the middle of the tunnel and stopped shortly after, leading absolutely nowhere. This tunnel was eerily quiet, as there was no sign of bats or other creatures. Levi held the torch out in front of him and high in the air to light the way. "There is something up ahead, but I can't make out what it is," Levi said, holding the torch high above his head trying to see in the distance. Even with the torch, it was difficult to see down the dark tunnel. As they were a little more than halfway down the shaft, the boys heard something fall behind them, and they both looked back. "What was that?" Levi said in a panicked shiver. Suddenly, a sizzling and crackling noise was heard and was becoming more pronounced by the minute.

"Do you smell smoke?" Jones asked in his trancelike meditative state.

"Yeah, I do," responded Levi. They quickly looked forward and discovered the Levi accidentally lit something hanging down from the top of the tunnel. "Oh no! What did I do?" a now freaked out Levi yelled. Upon looking farther down the tunnel, they saw many red wooden boxes with white letters that said "TNT." "Oh no! I think I...I think I lit a fuse! Run!" Levi screamed at the top of his voice as he dropped the torch and pulled Jones back toward the entrance.

The fuse was burning fast and created a heavy smog as it sped up toward the TNT. Levi and Jones were running at top speed to get out of the tunnel. With only a few feet of fuse left to burn, the boys made it back to the entrance and started running into the other tunnel. The TNT exploded with exceptional force and shook the ground while firing bones, rock, and ash out of the right tunnel entrance. The explosion was intense and, as a result, violently collapsed the right tunnel entrance.

The boys, covered with dust and small stones, fell to the ground just after entering the left tunnel. "Holy cow, did you see that? We almost died. There is no way we can go back in there now. Are you all right?" Levi yelled at Jones.

"I think so. I think so. That was unexpected. We must continue" Jones replied.

"What are you? That was so scary. We almost died in there. You're like a frigging robot or something." Levi chimed back.

"I'm just fine, Levi. We must continue. This way. This way, Levi." Jones said, dusting himself off and motioning to keep going.

Levi took a moment to just stare at Jones and shake his head in amazement. He stood up and dusted himself off, then continued.

CHAPTER SIX

The left tunnel was like the right, with the exception that the walls were lined with blown-out torches. Even though the tunnel was very gloomy looking far ahead every time, the boys were close to one of the ancient lanterns. Then something mysterious happened; the torch lit. The farther the boys walked down the left entrance, the more torches self-ignited, illuminating their surroundings. As what seemed to be a common theme in these shafts, dense spiderwebs and dust lined the area. Chunks of crystallized ore stuck out of the walls of this tunnel, and they would glow from the reflection of the light from the torches. The shaft was long, cumbersome, and took some time to travel. The floor was uneven, and they had to crawl over enormous stones and fallen support timber.

As the fellas journeyed through this area, Levi had a constant look of worry on his face, looking everywhere for any surprises that could have popped out and introduced itself. Jones maintained his calm zombie-like disposition. They made their way to the end of the tunnel with no other disturbances, much to the relief of Levi. Now at the end of this passage, they arrived at what turned out to be another ancient corridor of some sort. Thick roots and jungle-looking vines hung down, partially covering the fifteen-foot-high carved stone that made up the triangular frame of the unfamiliar area. Hieroglyphics were painstakingly carved all over the stone frame. A huge bronze-colored metal door with three faces protruding out of it kept the boys from moving on. There was some old mining equipment lying around, but there were also bamboo spears, bamboo armor, and ancient shields made of bamboo covered with some animal skin lying around.

Upon moving closer to this new access, the torches in the tunnel behind them simultaneously blew out, and two torches hanging from mounts on the triangular entrance ignited. "What is this place?" Levi asked as he hunched down and picked up a colorful cracked mask made of rotting old wood. Jones looked around and was silent as he appeared at peace while sporting a goofy grin. "I remember in history class seeing stuff like this. It almost looks like Aztec-type things," Levi said while thinking out loud. He turned to Jones, "Jones! Hello! Are you all there?" Levi still put effort in trying to knock Jones out of his daydreaming trance.

Jones looked at Levi with an innocent smile and said, "We need to continue."

"How?" Levi asked, pointing to the large door, which had more hieroglyphics carved on it.

Jones looked at the three faces on the door and then concentrated on the strange words beneath them. "This is another puzzle," Jones said while looking at the door.

"What do those words say?" Levi queried as his face grew with a confused look.

The amulet around Jones's neck suddenly glowed bright green. The flames in Jones's eyes became brighter as he stared at the words on the door. A haunting, low, eerie moan filled the compact space, and a green spot appeared on the ground behind the boys. It inundated Levi with fear, and he moved behind Jones, hiding from the scary miner. As he watched the miner materialize, Jones continued to stare at the door as if nothing were happening behind him. Sand and stone rotated in a counterclockwise direction around the glowing spot, while a body levitated from within it. The miner was back and still had a tempered look on his face as he rose from the ground.

The foul-looking specter looked at Levi and slowly moaned, "I'm surprised you have made it this far. I have never been this deep in the mine." His mouth seemed to froth with excitement. "I can feel the power of the treasure as we get closer." Levi thought that something wasn't right as he looked over Jones's shoulder. "You must hurry and complete your quest, or you will meet an atrocious fate."

"We're stuck!" Levi yelled out. "We can't get past this door."

"Silence! I have put everything Jones needs to know in his head. Figure it out or die!" The ghostly specter moaned as he slowly disappeared back into the ground. The dirt and stones stopped rotating, and the green spot faded away.

Levi stopped crouching behind Jones and crept up to where the spot appeared. "I don't understand. Why doesn't he realize that we do not understand—" Levi said before Jones interrupted him by yelling, "I've got it!"

Levi turned around with a surprised look on his face. "You do?" he exclaimed.

"Yes!" Jones said while pointing to the words under the three faces on the door. He started speaking in tongues like he could understand the writings. "Alob candorfious anatolta vindenio deulum," Jones murmured as he read the words while pointing to them.

"What does that mean?" Levi asked as he moved closer to the door, studying the faces.

"In layman's terms, it says 'Cover the prosperous but beware,'" Jones answered.

"Cover the prosperous? Beware? What does that mean, and how do we do it?" Levi chimed in, wanting to leave.

Jones looked around the area. He spotted the colorful, cracked mask that Levi noticed before. "This is it! We need to place this mask over the face that is prosperous," Jones said as Levi returned the idea with, "Huh? Say what? Okay, but what does beware mean?"

Jones carefully grabbed the mask and stood in front of the door. The three faces protruding out of the door had unique expressions. The first face was glowing with a happy, smiling expression. The second face appeared like it was crying, and the third face looked like something confused it. They all had a bracket of some sort to hold the mask on the face.

Levi was growing impatient, as he just wanted to leave before anything else could happen. He grabbed the mask from Jones's hand and said, "Well, it's obvious that this guy is smiling because he is prosperous!" So with that, Levi placed the mask on the smiley face. Instantly, the ground shook violently! Rocks and debris were falling from everywhere, and soon enormous boulders fell, covering the entrance to the tunnel the boys exited from. The lads clung close to the door as boulders fell in sequence, getting closer and closer to the boys. The shaking stopped, and the last boulders that fell were only feet away from the boys and the door.

A panic-stricken Levi screamed out, "What just happened? We are going to die!"

Jones looked at Levi with his calm face and said, "Why did you grab the mask from my hands? I think I had it figured out."

"Why are you so calm?" Levi yelled. "We were almost crushed. I just want to get out of here."

"Stay calm, my dear friend. We will make it out of here. Unfortunately, you put the mask on the wrong face, and I fear if that mistake is made again, this is where our journey will end."

Levi looked directly above them, and he saw two huge boulders that, if they fell, would crush the boys. Then Levi just stared at Jones in wonderment. He never heard him speak like that before. "What's wrong with you, Jones?" Levi asked worriedly.

"I am fine. Let's figure this puzzle out," Jones returned. Jones stood in front of the door, grabbed the mask, and said, "Cover the prosperous." He studied the faces and was deep in thought when he said, "Why would a man who is prosperous look confused?" With that, Jones slowly placed the wooden mask on the face that was crying. "A man who became prosperous would be so happy he would be crying." A vibrating noise started, and with the theatrics of rumbling, dust and debris fell. The enormous bronze doors slowly slid open. Jones grabbed one torch and smiled at Levi.

With a sigh of relief on Levi's face, both boys slowly walked through the opening. This appeared to be a larger tunnel than the previous one, and the air was heavy because it was damp. The ceiling and walls were covered with vines and foliage. Water was slowly dripping from the leaves on the vines. *How can this be? Plants like these can't live underground, can they?* Levi thought. What the two adventurers didn't see were the large number of beady eyes that were looking at them through the dense vegetation. Scattered throughout the area were huge dull-white sacs that looked like eggs.

"Something isn't right," Jones said.

"What do you mean?" replied Levi.

"This seems too easy. I feel like I know where we are going, but it shouldn't be this easy." Jones answered back.

"Why would you wish for more terrible stuff to happen? We have almost died several times, and you're complaining? I'll take a simple way out any day, ov—" Levi said before the sudden sounds of conga drums beating in a melodic rhythm interrupted him. Levi had a look of surprise and panic on his face.

Jones smiled and calmly said, "I thought so."

Several torches on the wall hidden behind the vines ignited one at a time in unison with the drumbeats. The boys noticed that the tunnel was long and appeared that it would be just as difficult to traverse. They both looked around for the source of the drumbeats, and they both knew at the same time that the rhythm was coming from straight ahead. "No, no, no, no. Come on," Levi said with irritation.

"We need to continue forward and move quickly," Jones said without blinking an eye.

They slowly proceeded deeper into the passage, trying not to trip over the roots and vines that were spread sporadically on the floor. The longer they traveled in the tunnel, the louder the beating of the drums became. Levi noticed the frightening creature's eyes looking at them. "W-what the?" he stuttered as he became even more afraid. Jones's trancelike state focused his attention at the end of the tunnel, not the creatures overhead. Abruptly, the sound of faint chanting flowed with the rhythm of the drumbeats. "Huh? Where is that coming from?" Levi screeched as he looked around with great anxiety.

"I'm not sure," Jones said with a monotone voice.

They continued down the jungle-themed tunnel, with the chanting and drumbeats getting louder by the second. It was like sensory overload, as both boys noticed small spiders crawling out of holes on the floor and up the vines. Carefully, they continued to step over all the jungle obstacles that lay in front of them. Looking all around themselves, they walked slowly, taking care not to trip, fall, or interrupt anything. Instantly, out of nowhere, the drumbeats and chants sounded faster. Levi and Jones looked at each other and stopped in their tracks. "I wonder why those sounds are speeding up?" inquired Jones.

By this time, Levi's eyes were almost bugged out of his head. "I'm afraid to go on," Levi said in a quiet nervousness. Without warning, the drumming and chanting immediately stopped. "Uh oh, w-w-what's happening now?" Levi stuttered out.

"I'm not sure," Jones said with a relaxed voice.

Dead silence filled the tunnel except for the crackling of the torches as they burned. The boys were silent, watching all the eyes watching them. A hissing noise and sounds of scurrying interrupted the silence. "Huh, what is that noise?" Levi said as he started to sweat out of nerves. The hissing and scurrying started again and were slightly louder. The hissing noise continued once again, and this time, they could feel that ground tremble beneath their feet. Instantly, the tunnel came alive with hundreds, all the creepy-crawly creatures scurrying through different hidden holes. Bats, rats, spiders, and other bugs were scrambling to get out of the tunnel. The boys didn't move a muscle, but stayed in place watching the event unfold. "What are they doing?" Levi yelled.

"I think they are running away," replied Jones with a blank grin on his face.

"Running away from what?" Levi said, not wanting to know the answer.

The hissing and multiple sounds of scuttling grew in volume and sounded like it was closer. Without haste, the drumming and chanting started again in unison with the loud noise. Poof! All the torches blew out. Levi grabbed Jones's hand and huddled together. Louder and louder the drums, chants, scampering, and hissing became. The boys fell to their knees, while Levi closed his eyes out of extreme terror. The experience was like a horrible haunted house attraction that malfunctioned. Then suddenly, silence. In the quiet, one torch lit at a time, starting far down the tunnel. They ignited slowly while getting closer to the boys. After what seemed like hours, the final torch lit next to poor Levi and Jones.

"I don't understand what is happening," Levi said as he returned to his feet.

"All this craziness and for what?" Levi asked as he and Jones looked behind themselves at the same time. They heard a powerful hiss and hundreds of footsteps. Both boys' jaws dropped to the ground. Three feet from them and as wide as the tunnel was a large mutated millipede-looking monster staring at them both.

"Chik chik hisss," the annelid thundered as its hundreds of legs pushed it about. Jones grinned in a trancelike state.

"Ah!" Levi screamed as he could barely get a footing to run. "Jones, run!" yelled Levi as he and Jones raced down the tunnel.

The annelid pushed its way along the tunnel, and it pursued the boys with feverish haste as the rest of its body slid out of a hole in the ceiling. This monster was forty feet long and almost consumed the entire tunnel with its circumference. Its legs scraping the tunnel was as near-deafening as the horrible hissing and dragging noise exploding from the creature. The drums and chanting began again and became faster and faster as the boys ran deeper and deeper into the tunnel.

The underground creature was fast and closed on their trail as it spit poisonous fluid during the pursuit. Levi continued to scream, and they both ran as fast as they could, trying not to trip on the roots and vines on the floor. "Keep going, Jones!" Levi yelled, looking at Jones who was running but had a blank face and no expression.

The amulet Jones was wearing glowed as they ran. The green jewel increased in intensity by the second. "I wonder what that means?" an out-of-breath Jones bellowed as he slowed down his pace. Closer and closer, the giant millipede-looking creature was gaining on the boys as venom dripped from its freakish fangs. The drum beats and chants were becoming even louder. Levi noticed that they were running out of tunnel because there was a weird-looking wall ahead.

"Jones! T-t-tunnel! We are running out of it!" Levi screamed.

"That is a p-problem!" Jones said, still out of breath.

The drumming and chanting were so loud it was as if they were next to the source of the noise. The amulet flashed an ultra-bright green light. The vines glowed with electric green energy. The moaning started once again. The tunnel only had about a football field in length left. "No! The tunnel is ending!" cried Levi. The vines and the amulet flashed and switched to a bright-white brilliant firework display of sparks and crackling, forming in a vertical circle that followed between the boys and the beast. The hissing and scuffling became louder as the beast was gaining on them, leaving only inches to spare. About fifty feet of tunnel was left, and just before they were about to hit the dead-end wall, the wave of fireworks formed a solid sparking wall. With the end of the tunnel just feet in front of them, Levi and Jones dove to the ground. Right after they dove to the ground, the monstrous creature slammed into the magical barrier. It gave a last hiss and loudly exploded into a million bright stars and sparks. All became silent again.

The boys were spread out on the ground, lying on their stomachs right in front of the dead end. Coughing, Levi said, "Why is this happening? Are you okay? That was extreme!" Jones still looked dazed and didn't say much, but he was looking down at his shirt. The fireworks wall disappeared as fast as it manifested. The amulet Jones was wearing still pulsated intently, and a dot of green energy instantly started rotating on the ground just behind them.

Growing in brightness and circulation of dirt and stones, the miner's corpse slowly rose out of the energy and stared at the boys. His scowl was firm, and he looked even angrier than before. "I can't join you in a physical form because I've been cursed by these mines and caves. I can follow you with the power of the amulet. Wherever you go, I can follow you, and we can search for the treasure together. The amulet will protect you while on your quest." He howled, "Keep going or die!"

With fear in their eyes, the boys returned their attention to the dead-end wall, which appeared to have some wooden lever sticking out of the center. More ancient hieroglyphic carvings were etched into the wall. Chiseled pictures of men with spears sticking in them dancing around a fire covered the center of the wall just above the lever. Vines and dense spiderwebs partially covered the ancient writings. Jones moved some debris out of the way to focus on the carvings. "What does it all mean?" Levi asked while studying the wall.

Jones initially said nothing at first, but then answered, "I'm not sure about the pictures, but I know we need to pull this lever to continue."

The miner's scowl slowly turned into an evil grin. Slowly putting his ghostly hands together and tapping his fingers, he moaned, "Yes, pull the lever and get the treasure." He then raised his arms and slowly sank back into the electric green energy swirling on the ground as it shrunk in size.

"Is it me or is he getting scarier?" Levi proposed to Jones.

Jones just mumbled while concentrating on the wall. "We need to pull this lever to continue," Jones said calmly.

With a mighty pull of the lever, whirling noises filled the air. They slowly lifted the rock wall into the air with thick old rope running around old pulleys that secured it. Much to the boys' disappointment, there was yet another entrance to who knows where.

CHAPTER SEVEN

On the other side of the entryway was a small tunnel the boys could walk through, and it was musty and very warm. The humid air was very unpleasant, and the boys both struggled to move. More skeletons, pitchforks, ore, and equipment lay scattered throughout.

"Wow. It's hot down here," Levi complained as he and Jones rounded the corner from the new entrance. "Give me a minute. I have to pee," Levi said to Jones as he found a spot to relieve himself. Levi was nervous about the skeleton's bones lying on the ground because he remembered what happened to Jones when he relieved himself. Jones just silently stared off into the direction they were walking. The tunnel opened up into an extensive area. The path was thin and smooth, and lava surrounded both sides.

The earthly hotbox glowed with a flickering bright and dull red light like the flames in a fireplace as the boys saw yet another challenge. Upon further investigation, the area was filled with large pools of lava and red-hot lava falls of bubbling, smoking slag pouring down from thirty feet high above. The path was narrowing the farther they walked in this scorching cavern. "I believe we are supposed to walk this way," said Jones with a glazed look and a goofy grin shaping his face.

"What? Are you kidding me, Jones? It's like we are in an oven!" Levi chimed in, "We will burn up in here! There's got to be another way."

Jones looked at Levi with a blank stare on his face. "No, this is the way." Jones walked on as if there were no dangers present.

Levi reluctantly followed, saying to himself, "This is ridiculous."

The noise of hot lava flowing around them sounded like a continuous roar of thunder as smoke rose and slag percolated from the pools on either side of the path. Slowly they walked down the path, which had a few skeleton bones strewn throughout the length. Charred pitchforks and other mining equipment were scattered on the path. Every step they took left a footprint that smoked on the hot ash floor. Both boys wiped the constant sweat from their brows. "Good grief!" an overheated Levi said as he wanted to wring out the sweat from his wet shirt. Jones was profusely sweating too but said nothing in his trancelike state as he kept walking.

Out of nowhere, a loud deafening explosion silenced the noise from the lava, and the ground shook. "What's going on? Run, Jones!" Levi cried out as he noticed in his peripheral vision an enormous chunk of rock exploding from behind them, and a massive overflow of lava was consuming the path behind them. "Run!" screamed Levi as the lava flow was catching up to them.

"This way!" Jones murmured as he ran toward the end of the path.

There, at the end of the path, looked like an old mine elevator built with wood timber columns and thick twine rope tied to the top of it that elevated it to higher ground. The shaking intensified, and the lava flow and slag were hot on the boys' trail. They made it to the spiderweb-covered elevator, which had many animal skulls mounted all over it. They leaped onto the platform. "Up! Up! How do we make it go up?" Levi asked in a panic.

In a calm and somber voice, Jones said, "I think pulling this lever would help."

"Well, pull it!" Levi yelled as the lava was only feet away.

Jones pulled the dried-up wooden lever and, with the sounds of rubbing and crackling the platform, slowly rose as an enormous boulder to the left of it descended.

The lava was flowing faster than the platform was moving, and once it was about five feet off the ground, the lava flow had reached the timber columns and ignited them almost instantly. Levi looked down as the platform rose slowly and became horrified because the ignited timbers that held the platform were burning fast. "Faster!

Faster! Does this thing move any faster?" a frightened Levi said as he shook his friend, trying to break the trance that kept him so calm and zombie-like.

"No," Jones spoke in a monotone voice.

They didn't have much higher to go, but the timber columns burned even faster because they were dried out. Soon the flames reached the moving platform, and it burned on its way up. "Ah!" Levi screamed as he scrambled to stay away from the fire. Just as they reached the elevator's destination, the middle of the platform ignited, and the boys jumped to the ground on the higher level. Flames completely consumed the elevator right after, and it rapidly burned hot. They watched as the elevator burned and fell back down into the depths of the lava.

"Ah! What...we...," a panicked Levi cried in relief. Jones just stared in the air like nothing happened. Levi grabbed Jones and slapped him multiple times. "Wake up! Wake up! Wake up!" Levi cried, trying to stir up his friend. "Wake up, Jones!" Levi yelled with one final slap and upon contact with Jones's cheek a bright blue flame blew them back from each other. They both landed on their butts several feet away from each other. "Ugh! What happened?" Levi uttered, picking himself up off the ground. He crawled over to Jones, who looked asleep. He shook Jones, "Are you there? Jones! Jones!" Then suddenly, Jones opened his eyes. Coughing and dusting the dirt off himself.

"Why did you hit me? What's going on? Where are we?" Jones said, confused and unaware of his previous state.

"You're back!" an excited Levi said, almost cheering.

"Back from what? All I remember was being furious with the miner. Then everything went black," Jones continued.

"You were under some spell or something. That miner said he put all kinds of information in your head. You were acting crazy because when we faced serious dangers, you just had this stupid grin on your face—"

Jones cut him off by saying, "Hey! Hey! Hey! I'm not insulting you! I don't have a stupid..." Suddenly, a loud and vibrating moan filled the area, silencing Jones while in midsentence. A glowing green fog covered the ground, and something rose from the ground and hover near the boys. It was the miner. As he took form in front of the boys, he had the same angry scowl carved on his face.

Pointing at Jones, the miner moaned, "My patience is running out. You may be out of the trance, but you still know the location of the treasure. I need that treasure! Find it!" At this point, both Levi and Jones noticed that the amulet around his neck and the miner's neck pulsated in unison. The crotchety old miner seemed visibly more agitated and could not stand still. His expression rotated between discontent and anger.

"We are trying. We've almost died several times looking for it. This mine is hell. We just want to go home," Levi answered.

"Silence!" barked the miner. "You are getting close. I can feel it."

Jones just glared at the miner with his own look of discontent on his face. "Come on, Levi. Let's keep going," Jones said as he was pulling on Levi's arm to continue.

As they crawled past the ghostly miner, the specter moaned, "Retrieve it or stay here forever!" Then he slowly sank back into the ground.

Levi was gathering his bearings as Jones pulled his arm. "Where do we go now?" Levi mentioned as he finally stood on his feet.

Jones turned to look at Levi as Levi noticed the blue flames were back in Jones's eyes. Jones said, "I think we should go this way." With that, they continued to walk for a short while.

"Is that a light ahead?" Levi said as they were walking down the tunnel away from the destroyed elevator.

"I think it is!" Jones blurted out as they walked even faster.

"Look, it's daylight!" shouted Levi as they noticed an exit to the shaft. The boys ran to what appeared to be an exit from the shaft. Cautiously walking through the opening, they soon discovered that they were high up on a mountain. In front of them was a wide cliff. It was about forty feet long, and it led to another shaft entrance. Just above the cliff were heavy thick clouds, and the boys could see mini trees and animals at the bottom of the deep side of the cliff. In the center of the area lay another mangled mine track that led into the other entrance and several broken pitchforks and shovels lying everywhere. "There is no way off this cliff," Levi stated as he looked around, noticing no way of escape.

Looking over the edge of the cliff, Jones said, "You're right. There is no way off this cliff that has to be over one hundred feet down to the ground."

Both boys noticed that this outdoor space looked nothing like any place they have ever seen in their town before.

"We have to go back in the mine," Jones said with reluctant confidence.

"What?" Levi shouted. "Aw man, this is crazy! We are finally outside and we have to go back in?"

Jones just looked at Levi and nodded his head. Edging their way forward, something looked different about the new mine shaft entrance. It was darker, and an eerie steam-like vapor hovered above the ground. "I think we are getting close," uttered Jones as he slowly looked back at Levi, not realizing that the translucent blue flames in his eyes grew in intensity.

"Your...your eye, Jones. That flame in your eyes is getting brighter," whispered Levi in a fearful tone.

"Let's do this," Jones said, looking forward once again.

The boys slowly walked into the opening, and the area soon grew dark as they were leaving the daylight behind. Dark, hazy, dirty, and dingy were the best way to describe what they were seeing. Every six feet were old tree trunk columns and cracked beams, which kept the area from caving in on itself. Old, worn-out lanterns hung from every other beam but haven't been lit for over one hundred years because their fuel had long dried up. They could hear the sounds of hissing and pressure in the distance. Huge galvanized pipes bolted together lined the sides of the carved-out walls as they came out of the wall and went back in the wall every ten feet. Some pipes were leaking mysterious hot pressurized steam at points, and others discharged a glowing light-blue liquid that was dripping on the ground and ran down the length of the passage. Several rotting and rusting mine cars flipped on their sides lined this passageway. Oddly enough, there were only remnants of the mine track because at every point the blue fluid touched the tracks, they were melting and dissolving. "Look at this liquid, Jones. Look what it's doing to the tracks. Don't step on it. Be careful." said Levi, sensing Jones may know more about it.

"I have no intention of touching it!" a cautious Jones replied with a slightly worried look on his face.

The area became even creepier as the only light in the tunnel was emitting from the glowing blue liquid. While following the passage deeper into the earth, once in a while the boys were startled by a colony of bats flying by or horrendous spiders staring at them as they hung from their thick dusty webs. "I'm getting nervous, Jones. Don't you remember what happened the last time we were in a dark mine shaft?" Levi said as he avoided touching the fluid while they walked. Jones didn't respond. "Jones! Did you hear what I asked you?" piped up Levi.

Jones stopped dead in his tracks and slowly looked back at Levi, not murmuring a word. The blue flames in his eyes were so bright that Levi could barely see his pupils. He said in a slow, calm voice, "We are very close to the Shard of Chance. We must keep going."

"Shard of Chance? What is a Shard of Chance? Jones! Jones!" Levi said with great worry as his best friend returned to walking down the shaft.

The thin streams of the blue fluid puddled in areas of uneven ground. Some were so big that it forced the boys to leap over many of them. While jumping over one of the bigger puddles, Levi's heel accidentally touched the fluid. Instantly, the heel of his shoe smoked, almost melting. He fell to the ground yelling as he took off that shoe to inspect it. "Jeez! W-wow. My shoe!" he said in amazement of the situation. Once the shoe stopped smoking, he put it back on.

"We must hurry!" Jones bellowed.

Eventually, the boys made it to a large, high round dome-style cavern. The blue fluid stopped at the entrance of this area. The boys saw something that stunned them both.

CHAPTER EIGHT

This area was open and possessed a very smooth blanket of white sand that filled every inch of floor from corner to corner. Heavy spiderwebs were shrouded around the ceiling of this room, attaching every corner like a horrific nest of clutter. Located in the center of the area about fifty feet from where the boys were standing was a huge, partially submerged boulder sticking out like a sore thumb. Toward the center of this huge rock, a gigantic chiseled bright-glowing blue shard sticking three feet out of it. The light radiating out of the shard lit the entire cavern. The boys just stood there in awe as the blue shard emitted this powerful, strange light as it made a low pulsating bass noise.

As Levi moved toward the shard, Jones quickly grabbed him. "No! Don't walk toward it. Something is not right," explained Jones. He continued, "It seems too easy. Something is definitely not right."

"What do you mean something is not right? Let's go investigate that thing," Levi said as he took a step on the sand and his footprint sank into nothingness. The blue fluid that was flowing like a river in the tunnel filled the void where he had stepped. Jones quickly pulled him back since he still had ahold of him.

"I told you something isn't right. Don't walk on that sand!" yelled Jones.

"Where the...What the...where's the sand...my shoe? It filled up with that blue fluid in the place of my footprint," replied Levi.

"Don't move!" said Jones as behind the boys a swirling green mist appeared to rotate from the sand and slowly took the form of the miner as he rose from it once again. As the miner's shape was completing, both boys turned around to look. The evil scowl and anger of the miner was clear. The amulet was glowing even brighter as it appeared to be rotating on its chain.

He looked down at the boys, and with a slow, stretched-out moan, the miner said, "You're so close. Can you feel its power?" As he looked around and floated over to the blue shard in the center of the cavern, his eyes became focused on the shard as he raised his hands over it as if trying to touch it. Little white stars floated to and from the miner's hands and the shard. "Yes, you're very close. I can feel it. What's taking you so long? You must figure out how to get to the treasure. I can feel its power. The end is near. You must figure out how to touch this shard to continue. Its power is glorious. It grows stronger the closer we get, it's here."

"We can't walk across this sand. It breaks apart and turns into that blue slag that almost ate my shoe," spoke up Levi as he looked at the miner with curiosity.

"That is not my problem. You accepted the quest, and you must figure out how to get the treasure," interrupted the miner. "Time grows short, make haste or suffer the consequences!" With that last warning, the miner appeared to vaporize, then disappeared back into the ground.

"Now what are we supposed to do?" barked Levi as he panicked. "I just want to go home and we are stuck in this mess, and I—"

Jones raised his hand to Levi's face, almost instantly silencing him. "This is just another puzzle we need to figure out." A calm Jones continued, "We can't walk across the sand because we will sink in that blue muck. The shard is too far away for us to jump on it. Hmmmm."

Both boys sat down Indian style on the edge of the eerie sand. Levi had his hands balled up in a fist and resting on his cheeks, while Jones sat in a meditative state. "I don't get it!" uttered Levi. "If we walk on the sand, we sink and get eaten up from this blue stuff, yet we have to make it to the crystal and touch it to get out of here! I just don't get it."

In his meditative state and with blue flames still flickering in his eyes, Jones said, "I'm not sure either. But we have to figure this out."

Levi interrupted, "Well, we have nothing to build like a bridge or something to walk on to get to that crystal. I just—"

"Wait!" shouted Jones, "That's it! We need to travel across something to get there. But what?"

Levi shouted, "Jones! Are you in the same place with me? How can we make anything? There is nothing but sand, spiders, and this blue muck. We are never..."

Suddenly, Jones's eyes rolled to the back of his lids, and he trembled. The blue flames in his eyes became very intense and glowed the same color as the blue sludge that was glowing and bubbling as it boiled. The amulet around his neck glowed. His mouth fell open as if he were trying to say something. Levi scooted back and stared in awe, afraid of what was happening to his friend. Jones slowly rose and levitated three feet about the ground. The blue sludge under the sand boiled violently. The spiders on the ceiling scurried away in unison as fast as they could.

An echoing moan made its way out of Jones's mouth as the sludge steamed. The bubbles were taking shape as they rose from the depths. Gradually, six glowing ghost-like forms of different miners rose from the sludge. They were slightly translucent, and all had tools in their hand. As if watching in slow motion, one miner raised a pickax and drove it downward into nothing. "Ching!" was the noise made. The rest of the ghosts followed suit, raising their pickaxes and swinging them down. Ching! Ching! Ching! Levi looked in horror as this magical spectacle took place. The sounds of bubbles and boiling filled the area. As the ghost continued to swing the axes, a translucent blue piece of track seemed to form out of thin air. The ghostly men continued swinging axes and building what looked like a ghostly bridge to the crystal.

The apparitions' swinging of the pickaxes picked up in speed. Once the track was complete, forming out of thin air, the miners started bringing wood, metal, and wheels over close to Levi. Poor Jones was still levitating in the air and moaning. Levi couldn't bring himself to say anything as the specters assembled all those pieces into a mine car. The ghosts feverishly assembled the mine car. As fast as it started, it ended. The glowing blue mine car was complete and ready for the boys. As fast as the miners materialized, they melted back into the bubbling blue sludge. Jones descended to the ground while returning to his conscious self.

"What? What happened?" Jones asked.

"You were floating again...there were more ghost miners...and now this track!" cried Levi.

Jones looked over to the ghostly mine car and tracks. "We must get in!" Jones said.

"Something told me you would say that. Come on." Levi sighed as he slowly climbed in the paranormal skip, followed by Jones. Soon after the boys entered the mine car, it started to move forward toward the blue shard. As the car progressed down the track, the blue ooze boiled again. Steam and bubbles erupted through the sand, and a horrible moaning noise began. "What's going on?" Levi screeched.

"I'm not sure, but I wasn't expecting this," answered Jones as he looked around.

The moaning became louder as many ghostly hands reached out of the ooze. Ghastly-looking ghouls rose from under the track. They looked like the previous miners but much scarier. Their faces were without eyes, and their mouths hung open, crying the eerie moan that filled the room. "Ah!" Levi shrieked as the ghostly vehicle edged closer to the shard. The ground was disappearing under a mysterious fog that seemed to form out of nowhere. Jones had a look of worry on his face but remained calm in that moment. "Faster, faster! How do we go faster?" Levi screamed as the ghouls tried to grab them.

Focused on the shard, Jones said, "Almost there. Almost there."

Levi was dodging the grasping hands of the ghosts trying to reach in the cart, while Jones showed no interest in anything but the shard.

Just before they reached the radiating shard, the old miner had materialized out of the fog and levitated in the air from the blue ooze muck that boiled below and stared at the boys with his teeth clenched right before they were close enough to touch the shard. The amulet was intensely bright and pulsating. "Yes...yes... Can you feel the power...?" he moaned out eerily, "Quickly, touch it! Touch the shard!"

Jones held his arm out straight and firm with his index finger pointing forward. The mine car continued to creep forward, getting ever so closer to the shard. Suddenly, shortly after reaching the middle of the track and very close to the shard, the mine car stopped. "What's happening?" Levi said with rage as he dodged spiritual bullying from the rising ghost.

Observing the situation, Jones looked at Levi and said, "We have to jump to reach the shard. I seem unable to move."

"Jump? Jump?" Levi said, dodging ghostly hands. "What do you mean you're stuck?" Levi pointed to the bottom of the mine car, which had blue fluid leaking in the bottom. The track and bridge were sinking into the sand and blue abyss. "You've got to be kidding me!" Levi said as he observed the blue muck was surrounding Jones's shoes, almost disabling his movement. Levi looked forward and had a minor anxiety attack. "Okay. Okay. I can do this," Levi said, analyzing the distance to touch the shard. "I can't believe I'm doing this," Levi said as he took a breath and jumped from the mine car to the shard. He landed on top of the shard but lost his footing and almost fell into the mucky blue sand.

"Touch the top of the shard," Jones said in a calm voice as the mine car was consumed.

"Give me your hand!" Levi yelled to Jones as he held his hand out. Jones grabbed his hand and pulled him onto the shard as the mine car completely sank into the ooze below. After several seconds, both the mine car and tracks were gone.

CHAPTER NINE

Levi turned his attention to the shard from which they still clung. He reached his arm up high and barely touched the top of the shard when suddenly they heard a rumble of noise filling the chamber. Both boys were looking around, searching for the source of the noise. As if a jack-in-a-box suddenly opened instantly, thousands of flies, bugs, and hornets forced their way into the chamber through multiple hidden holes in the wall. Levi, surprised, fell off the shard and landed on his back at the base of the shard while covering his face. The amulet around Jones's neck glowed intensely. The chamber became full of these swarming pests flying around the boys like a hurricane. In a circular motion, as if it were water flushing down the toilet, all the sand in the area moved in a rotating motion around the base of the shard. In a nonpanic-stricken mode, Jones fell off the shard. The boys struggled to stay above the sand by flailing their arms and legs about. "Help, Jones! Help!" Levi cried out.

They slowly but surely, through the horrifying sound and churning action of the sand, sank and oozed down through the sand to an area below the shard. They fell about ten feet from the ceiling to the cavern floor below, landing on another soft area of sand. They ended up in a secret chamber not seen for hundreds of years. This was a strange place to Levi and Jones. It didn't look like any of the other areas that the boys had encountered so far. A multitude of rock formations lay in this area, along with small pools of water. Gigantic roots, odd plants, broken pottery, and dense spiderwebs surrounded the area, covering the ceiling and walls.

The floor was covered partially with dirt and bones, which covered an ancient, beautifully tiled floor that was built in a path that led to the end of the hallway-style room. The tile had antiquated depictions of an archaic society's existence. Rock formations surrounded the tile floor on either side and continued till the room almost ended. Anyone could easily mistake this area for a creepy tomb. Making the ground more difficult to traverse were the hundreds of skeletons lying around for almost one hundred feet. The skeletons were positioned in their ultimate resting place, as they were still holding rusted weapons and rotting shields as if they were still guarding what lay ahead. The boys sat where they fell and were trying to look around the bleak area when random ancient torches suddenly ignited in sequence and lit the area.

"Where are we now?" Levi said while dusting off.

"This is the chamber we need to be in. It's here!" bellowed a monotone Jones.

"What's here?" questioned Levi, looking around.

"The treasure," Jones said as he pointed to the opposite end of the chamber. Across the endless dead bodies and light haze in the air appeared to be what the boys were looking for on the far side of the chamber. Levi and Jones stood up and sauntered down the corridor, working hard to avoid falling on the root-laden floor and climbing over all the fallen dead. They cringed as they moved past dozens of skulls that were staring at them mostly with their jaw wide open or, should you say, those that still had a lower jawbone attached.

They carefully watched where they stepped, as they didn't want to step on or disturb the bones of the carcasses. "T-this is scary, Jones," Levi whispered as they trudged one step at a time down the hallway. Jones still carried a blank look on his face as they inched their way forward, trying not to step on any bones. It felt like hours to the boys as they calmly made their way closer to the end of the path. They both concentrated on looking around the area so they wouldn't set off any more hidden traps. There, surrounded by bleak gray and bronze rock formations, lay an old chest mostly surrounded by and locked into place by the stones and minerals that were plentiful in the chamber.

Mostly covered in cobwebs, Jones stepped forward and stood on an elevation of broken stones. He gently pushed aside the webbing, watching for booby traps and discovered that what he thought was just a regular strongbox was really an elegant, elaborately detailed treasure chest, which was glowing from the solid polished copper from which it was made. The boys were in awe to see something this beautiful in such a place as this. Rare gems and fiery opal stones lined the metal bands that held the old chest together. The boys noticed that the large golden lock speckled with etched diamonds secured the lid, but had no keyhole. "That's odd. I mean, I know we don't have a key, but there is nowhere to put one." Levi said as he observed Jones holding the lock in his hand.

They sat there for a short while, pondering what to do next when Jones's amulet pulsated from a dull glow to a bright flash. "What's happening?" Levi asked, afraid that some other trap was activated.

"I'm not sure," Jones uttered.

The amulet gradually pulsated from a low tone to an even louder hum while growing even brighter. A haunting, low moan filled the silent chamber as the boys looked around for the source. A gentle breeze consumed the room.

"Not again!" shouted Levi.

"I don't know what's going on," said Jones with no fear on his face.

Back in the center of the hallway-like room, a bright green spot materialized and resonated in the middle of the tile path and pulsed and rotated on the floor. The breeze turned into a powerful wind. The boys both fell farther down the rock mound while trying to hold on to the chest. All the dirty old and tired bones of the dead shook and vibrated in place. Soon they began to fly in the air as if a cyclone were sucking everything into the green spot, which appeared on the path. Both boys could say nothing as they watched in terror as it sucked the bones into the green spot, which morphed into a sizeable hole that had green light beaming out of it. A horrifying, spectral, gargantuan body slowly emerged from the spot as fast as bones were being sucked into it. This was not a full ghostly apparition. Instead, it was a full living body of the miner, and he stood eight feet tall. The glowing veins in his arms were pulsating in rhythm with the amulet around Jones's neck. His teeth were clenched with drool dripping off his crusty, cracked lips. His eyes were closed until his feet hovered above the hole.

The miner's evil eyes opened with a horrifying glare. He looked at the boys as he painted an evil grin on his rough face and gave a haunting laugh. The wind slowly died down, and most of the bones in the room had disappeared to give the miner his body. "It is almost complete," murmured the miner as he salivated while looking forward.

Levi gained his composure and said, "W-what's almost complete?"

The miner slowly pointed at the chest. "Open the chest now!" howled the miner as his evil scowl became more menacing.

"How?" Levi stammered. "There is no keyhole in the lock."

"Take the amulet off Jones and place it against the lock," said the miner in an evil and eerie echoing voice as he pointed to Jones. Levi and Jones looked at each other in fright.

"Something is not right," Jones said as he slowly removed the amulet from his neck and started inching it closer to the lock. The miner's eyes opened wide and the look of extreme intensity molded his face.

"What do you mean something isn't right?" replied Levi.

"Well, look at him. This isn't the guy we first met down here," chimed in Jones.

"Hurry!" yelled the miner. Both boys jumped from the sudden outburst. The closer Jones was to the lock, the brighter the amulet glowed, and little green orbs floated around it in a circular pattern. "Faster, faster!" yelled the miner as he visually shivered and salivated with excitement.

Suddenly, Levi grabs Jones's hand, stopping him from touching the lock. "Hold on!" Levi yelled, looking at the miner, "When we open this lock, how do we know that you won't hurt us and we can go back home?"

The miner's eyes turned red as if a fire were lit behind them. He balled up his fist and clenched his teeth till a few of them cracked. "If you don't open the chest, I will finish you here! It's almost complete!" shouted the miner as he swayed around in anger.

Levi looked back at Jones. "I don't trust him either, but it looks like we have no choice." Levi removed his hand from Jones, and Jones carefully raised the amulet and touched the lock. A bright flash of green light blinded the boys as the amulet came in contact with the lock. The ground shook, and the amulet faded away and returned to Jones's neck.

Jones appeared to be out of the trance and acted like himself again. He looked around in surprise and said, "W-What's going on? Where are we?" Slowly, the lock creaked opened with a rusty grinding noise and fell off the chest, releasing some diamond dust.

"It is done! Hahahaha. Finally, after all these years, I have it!" the miner shouted.

Levi and Jones looked at each other, trying to figure out what that meant. The lid of the chest slowly squeaked open. The boys' eyes opened wide as the lid was rising. When the lid was a few inches open above the chest, a bright glassy white orb gradually floated out the chest and traveled to the very back of the room while making a humming sound. All other noises became silent as the orb floated about. The temperature cooled down significantly. Once again, the boys had to cover their eyes as the brightness of the orb grew in intensity. "What is that?" Jones said to Levi as they watched the orb float behind the chest. The luminous white ball broke apart and transformed into the shape of a man.

The older, nonthreatening-looking man wore half-armor and half-aged garments fashioned together from different animals. Upon his head, he donned a headdress made of feathers, antlers, and copper. His shoes appeared to resemble enormous bear paws. He was a timeworn tribal guardian. "What is going on?" howled the miner with a look of surprise on his marred face. When the brightness of the transformation dulled away, the guardian looked at the boys. "Who are you?" moaned the miner.

"Igmar mo tazafran shuly," said the apparition.

"What is this language you speak?" the miner taunted.

Jones looked at Levi and said, "I don't understand him. Do you?"

Levi shook his head and looked back toward the apparition.

"I don't have time for this!" the miner yelled out.

"Silence!" the solid spirit mass said as his face turned angry looking at the miner. "I will now speak your dialect. I am Yoshdamya (Yo-sha-da-my-a), the sacred guardian of the contents of this chest. I have long waited for this day for many millennia. What you seek in this chest possesses unfathomable power—"

"And it's mine!" interrupted the miner as he lunged forward with his hand extended, as he wanted to grab the treasure.

Instantly, a burst of brilliant light filled the room and, with a firework's crackle, knocked the miner back several feet and stunned him as the guardian yelled, "Back!"

Levi looked at the guardian with plenty of fear and innocence in his eyes before pleading, "We have been through so much. We were trying to escape a storm when we met this miner who forced us here. We have almost died trying to get whatever is in this chest. Please tell us what it is so we may go home."

The guardian nodded and then spoke, "Millions of years ago, this pious planet had very few lifeforms roaming on it. There grew a single tree high in elevation in the middle of nowhere. The environment was harsh, as there was very little water, yet this tree grew very strong. It glowed with a pale white light and stood tall while extending many branches. No vegetation could grow within fifty fathoms of this sacred tree. As time passed, a forest grew around the tree, but no root could disturb its boundaries. Weather of all kinds never hurt the tree as it grew massive. Some have said that its leaves touched the heavens. Neither fog nor cloud could keep the sunlight from shining on it. Years of earthquakes and other natural disasters could not uproot this hallowed hardwood entity. Over several thousand years, as man developed, he grew insane from the mystery of the sacred tree. Even though they tried, they could not get close enough to harvest or harm it. Animals would live near the base of the tree, and it would protect them, but not man. Stories would be told for centuries about its legacy and power."

Suddenly the miner opened his eyes and stood back up. "Enough of this! Give me the treasure!" ordered the miner as he raised his hand, and some loose chunks of rock nearby flew at the guardian. Instantly, a bright flash of light filled the room and a thunderous crackle exploded.

"Back!" yelled the guardian. The flying rocks flew back toward the miner, knocking him down and stunning him again. He continued with the legend, "One day, there was an ancient tribesman who disguised himself hiding under bear fur to fool the tree, and he got close enough to the tree to touch it, but when he did, his tribe never saw him again. Man called this ancient timber the Tree of Time, planted here from beings from beyond this world. It existed here for millions of years until one day, a great fiery ball fell from the sky, and the ground opened and swallowed it up. The tree's glow would flicker as if it were hurt. It soon lost its ability to protect itself as it was slowly sinking into the ground. There was always someone watching the area, and at the time it was sinking into the ground, a tribesman ran to the tree and chopped a small piece off the root before it vanished forever. This man ran off, never seen again."

Suddenly, the chest opened all the way up. Inside the chest was a thick thatch of spiderwebs, but also inside the chest was a lining made of bright-glowing golden cloth. What was lying inside surprised the boys. "What in the world is that?" Levi said, pointing to the contents.

"It looks like a stick," Jones responded.

Positioned deep in the middle of the chest was a dirty, knotty, thick piece of wood with a slight curve in the middle that was being held up by two eagle claws. It was about fourteen inches long and still carried the smell of the ground it once grew in. "Is this what we went through all of this nightmare for?" Levi yelled to the miner, who was regaining his consciousness.

"It is a piece of the root from the Tree of Time," said the guardian.

"It's mine, and I'm taking it now!" an enraged and fiery glowing miner said as he lunged forward again.

"Back!" the guardian yelled as another bright flash of light knocked the miner back yet again, this time stunning him good. The stick slowly rose and floated above the chest while rotating in a circle. "This root is all that is left from the tree, and it contains substantial powers. Although all of its total powers are unknown, I'm sure you will discover more of its secrets. Its primary function gives its protectors the ability to bring a small segment of time to the holder," the chest keeper pointed out. Levi and Jones looked confused.

"What do you mean it can bring time to the holder?" Jones asked.

"Where ever you are on earth, you can summon the root to bring forth the living shadows of the past that happened in that area," explained the guardian.

"Oh, I get it!" said Levi. "If we were standing somewhere in the city of, say, Detroit, we could use the root to show us what happened in history before Detroit was ever a city."

"You have the wisdom of a man ten times your age. The root gives you the power to alter time's shadow, and when you're around it long enough, your body may absorb some of its magic. You cannot stop time, as it has to run its natural flow and progression into the future." He paused then continued, "Now listen, young guardians, as this is very important. Whenever there is stress in the flow of time, the root will summon you to wield its power to promote good and just deeds. With this power comes a great and difficult responsibility." The guardian continued, "If you call a piece of time from its natural path, you must put it back after you're done or horrible things will happen. As the new guardians of the root, it will attach to you, and only you will be able to use its power till another guardian is eventually found."

"But hold on, if it has powers that its protector can use, why are you stuck guarding it in a chest?" Jones asked.

"I took a vow to protect the root until you two found it," said the guardian as the boys looked at him with shock on their faces.

"What?!" Jones said in shock.

"Us two?" Jones continued.

"Yes, you two." The guardian continued, "Everything in time happens for a reason, and it was foretold many millennia ago that two young guardians from the future named Levi and Jones would find the root and protect it." The boys' eyes opened very wide, and their jaws hung open with this news.

The miner finally came to and was angrier than ever. He stood up, and it appeared he was concentrating all his energy on his next attempt. "Don't touch it! Move!" the miner yelled as he used his powers to push the boys out of the way. He waved his hand, and enormous boulders levitated and shot toward the guardian who disappeared when the boulders hit him. He then grabbed the root from its floating point. Both boys scrambled off to the side of the mound that held the chest. He turned around and glared at Levi and Jones and the guardian who reappeared. "This simple little stick will give me unlimited power! It can alter time, and I can go back and make myself unbelievably rich and powerful. Now I can leave this mine for good." The miner laughed as he clutched even tighter onto the root and continued to glare at the boys.

"What do you mean?" shouted Jones.

The miner looked at Jones and said sarcastically, "Oh, I'm sorry. Didn't I introduce myself? I'm really Orville Crenshaw, self-proclaimed philanthropist, renowned archaeologist, and soon-to-be most powerful being on earth. I discovered the rumored legend about this root over one hundred years ago. You so-called guardians just helped me collect the once mythical and most powerful treasure of all time!"

"What!? You lied to us?" Levi said.

"Those idiot miners couldn't do the job, and I was stuck here, but you two gullible little children put it right in my hands," uttered Crenshaw. "It's time for you to die!" said Crenshaw as he waved the root at the boys.

Suddenly the guardian raised his staff. "Back!" the guardian yelled as he conjured the bright light that knocked the miner off his feet before. The miner dropped the root as it knocked him far back. As the boys scrambled to get the root, Crenshaw stood up and started chanting an incantation. His eyes turned evil red and glowed with furious fire. The ground started shaking, and the hole from whence he came started growing wider. They could hear wailing spirits as the hole grew in size. The ground was shaking so violently the boys couldn't make it to their feet.

Both boys were panic-stricken. "No! You said we could leave when we found it!" yelled Levi as he almost soiled himself.

"There is no way you're getting out of here, and you will be trapped here for all time!" yelled Crenshaw as skeletons from the ancient guards started crawling out of the hole. Shortly later, the hole closed up.

Standing in front of the boys at full evil attention were fifty skeletons partially covered in ancient robes and primeval armor. Their eyes glowed with a piercing green light as they clinched their many missing teeth. Crenshaw used his power to levitate the root and bring it back to his hand. "Enough games! It's time for you to die!" And with a wave of his hand, Crenshaw ordered the skeleton army to attack.

In unison, they all raised their spears, swords, and shields and charged at the boys. A horrendous moan and howling echoed from the skeletons' mouths as they started throwing their spears and waving their swords about. Levi and Jones grabbed each other in fear and held tight. The guardian waved his staff, and as soon as the closest skeleton approached the boys, a bright flash and loud crackle sounded, but nothing happened as the skeletons still charged for the boys. The guardian had a grim look of surprise on his face. Crenshaw laughed a haunting laugh and yelled, "You can't stop me! I will be all-powerful and control time." He extended his arm, and the root hovered above his hand and rotated clockwise as it pulsated with energy.

The guardian looked at the boys and said, "I'm sorry. I can't protect you from the powers of the root." He held his staff high and tried to fend off the magic of Crenshaw, but he was losing.

"I am all-powerful! You have done my bidding, and now you will suffer an untimely death," he said with his diabolical laugh as he raised the spinning root and pointed it at Levi and Jones. "There is nothing you can do! I'm indestructible! Now die!" Crenshaw yelled out as a beam of deadly magic shot from the root toward Jones and missed. Jones jumped back in fear, and he and Levi hid behind a boulder. The room continued to shake, and it was very hard for Levi and Jones to stay hidden. Crenshaw held his hand out again as the root spun above it. Another wave of magic shot toward the boys, and the boulder they were hiding behind crumbled into small rubble.

The guardian summoned all his strength and yelled, "Back!" as a more powerful flash of light finally knocked Orville back several feet, causing him to drop the root.

Once again Crenshaw extended his hand and, with his magic, pulled the root toward him with evil intent. The boys were running back and forth trying to dodge the root's power. This continued a few more times as Crenshaw tried to kill poor Levi and Jones. As the shaking continued, more rocks and boulders broke from the chamber and nearly missed the tired youth. "Run!" Levi yelled, pulling Jones toward the chest. By that time, Crenshaw was back to his feet with the root still spinning above his hand and shot another powerful wave of magic toward the boys. Jones tripped and started falling backward. As that happened, the wave of magic hit the amulet around his neck and reflected with the same intensity back toward Orville.

"No!" screamed the specter. When the magic hit Crenshaw in slow motion, his body exploded into millions of brilliant stars, while the root fell back to the ground. Both Crenshaw and the amulet around Jones's neck disappeared.

The ground shook more violently. The guardian extended his hand, and a trail of white sparks shot toward the root and brought it back to Jones's hand. Levi and Jones looked at the guardian who said, "My time here is done, and now I can rest. The root is yours to protect now. Use it wisely. Use it for good. Never let it fall into evil hands." He then faded away. The ground was breaking apart as it shook more violently. Rocks were breaking free from the walls of the chamber. Jones stood up and grabbed Levi as both were trying not to get hit from the falling debris.

"How do we get out of here?" screamed Levi, clutching onto Jones. The room shook even more vigorously. Cracks formed on the ceiling and walls. Water soon rushed from the cracks of the collapsing walls and started submerging the floor. Boulders were falling just feet from the boys. Water was up to their waist and getting deeper.

"Hold on to me!" yelled Jones as he struggled to hold the root in the air. The water was now up to their shoulders when, almost instantly, the root glowed bright white and spun above Jones's fingers, which were almost submerged. The boys were underwater except for the root spinning just above it. A large boulder directly above the boys broke free and was about to crush them underwater when a blinding flash of sparkling light exploded from the root, rendering everything instantly dark and silent.

Everything was nothing. Everything was black, and everything was silent. For an instant, nothing seemed to exist. When Levi opened his eyes, he was back in his classroom before they were dismissed. The regular noise of a busy classroom continued as if nothing ever changed its course. Levi looked around the classroom at all the other students, then he looked across the room and saw Jones who was looking back at him. They both stared at each other in amazement as the background noise seemed to muffle life's reality. Levi, staying silent, read Jones's lips as he was saying, "What just happened?" Levi looked around and shrugged his shoulders. He mouthed back, "I don't know!"

The school bell rang earlier than usual as it was a half day that started the three-day weekend. Mrs. Barren, one of the few English teachers, closed her textbook, which was lying on top of her desk, and said, "Okay, everyone, class is dismissed. Enjoy your weekend and study for next week's test." Every student in the room was full of excitement and cheered while gathering their books and bags and while starting to walk out to the school buses. They could hear current music playing from various Bluetooth speakers and head-phones. The hallway was filled with kids closing their lockers, and they heard unwavering enthusiasm as most were excited to leave early that Thursday morning.

Levi and Jones walked out of the classroom and through the busy hallway. "Are we...are we dreaming?" Levi asked with a puzzled look on his face.

"I don't have a clue. I don't think so," replied Jones, who was just as shocked as his best friend.

While the students were scrambling around the schoolyard looking for their bus or ride home, some staff members and chaper-ons were looking out toward the ocean past the school buses, view-ing the horizon. It was a beautiful day, and the sun reflecting off the gentle waves of the ocean was awe-inspiring and brought peace and tranquility to the minds of all who pondered.

"This is some wicked déjà vu," Jones said as he and Levi slowly walked next to each other toward the buses.

"But there was a storm brewing. What happened? This isn't what happened before," Levi answered back.

"It must have been the root. We must have flashed back before anything ever happened." Jones acknowledged.

"But it happened," Levi interrupted. "The caves, the water, the monsters, that miner! It was all real, wasn't it?"

The boys chuckled in confusion and boarded the bus.

"We aren't crazy, Levi. It was all very real. It seems like a dream, but it had to be real. We must be in a different reality where the storm never happened," said Jones.

The bus soon departed and, within a few miles, started drop-ping off students at their regular stops. "Well, if it was a dream, that was one heck of an adventure." Levi said just as the bus hit a pothole and the root stuck out of his bag. "What the?" Levi said in shock.

"Shhhh!" Jones interrupted as he whispered, "See? See? It wasn't a dream. There's the root."

Levi quickly stuffed it back in his bag before any of the remaining students on the bus noticed.

Soon after, the bus stopped in front of Levi's house. The boys exited the bus, and Levi stood there for a moment after the bus pulled away. He looked around at the neighboring homes and noticed that many residents were busy walking around outside and tending to their daily activities. The waves of the ocean were flowing with normal movement, and the many types of birds were flying around as if they had no intention of going anywhere else. He invited Jones into his house, and they went straight to the kitchen counter where Levi opened his bag to look at the root. Just then, his mom opened the front door.

"Hi, honey. I'm home early." Levi's mother gestured to him. She continued, "Hey, Jones, how are you doing?"

"Oh, I'm great, Mrs. Lumboss," Jones answered as he covered the open backpack up, hiding the root.

"I have such exciting news, Levi. I've worked so hard, and it finally paid off. I just accepted a promotion to be a full-time travel blogger for the travel company I work for, and I get to venture all around the world and write about the destinations we sell in the office. You know, Levi, it's almost summer vacation. Your father and I have been saving up some money, and well, how would you like to join me on a vacation to a different country for the summer? Wouldn't that be exciting? Jones, I'm sure your mother would let you join us," she said as she walked into a different room. "Imagine the fun and adventures that we could have experiencing other cultures and cuisines," she continued.

Jones opened the bag a little so only he and Levi could see the root. He and Levi gave each other a huge grin.

Levi said, "That sounds great, Mom. We can't wait."

ABOUT THE AUTHOR

Ryan Crawford is a Grand Rapids, Michigan, native and college graduate from NIT and alumni of Davenport University. His passion for adventure and travel inspires him creatively, resulting in this book and many more to come.

His passion for exploring new cultures, cuisines, and destinations gives him a unique perspective into other spirited individuals who enjoy the power of storytelling.

With his imagination running wild and free, he writes in a way that will captivate and make people that much more enthralled. He has many more stories to share with you, so stay tuned and enjoy the ride.